D1586879

The item should be retu
by ⁄

MARIO BENEDETTI

Springtime in a Broken Mirror

Translated by Nick Caistor

PENGUIN BOOKS

PENGUIN CLASSICS

UK | USA | Canada | Ireland | Australia
India | New Zealand | South Africa

Penguin Books is part of the Penguin Random House group of companies
whose addresses can be found at global.penguinrandomhouse.com.

First published as *Primavera con una esquina rota* 1982
This translation first published in Penguin Classics 2018
001

Copyright © Fundación Mario Benedetti, c/o Schavelzon Graham Agencia
Literaria, www.schavelzongraham.com
Translation copyright © Nicholas Caistor, 2018

The moral right of the author and translator have been asserted

Set in 11.25/14 pt Dante MT Std
Typeset by Jouve (UK), Milton Keynes
Printed in Great Britain by Clays Ltd, St Ives plc

A CIP catalogue record for this book is available from the British Library

ISBN: 978–0–241–32720–3

In memory of my father (1897–1971), who was a chemist and a good man.

If I knew I were to die tomorrow
And spring came the next day
I would die happy
Because it was the day after tomorrow.

Fernando Pessoa

Out-of-date calendar, broken mirror.

Raúl González Tuñón

Intramural
(Tonight I am alone)

Tonight I am alone. My cellmate (one day you'll know his name) is in the sick bay. He's a good guy, but sometimes it's not such a bad thing, being alone. I can think more clearly. I don't have to screen myself off to think of you. You'll say that four years, five months and fourteen days is too long to spend just thinking things over. And you're right. But it's not too long to spend thinking of you. The moon is shining, and I'm making the most of it, writing to you. It's like a balm, the moon, it always calms me. And its light, however faint, shines on the paper, which is important because at this time of night they cut off the electricity. I didn't even have moonlight, though, for the first two years, so I'm not complaining. As Aesop concluded, there's always someone worse off than you. A lot worse off, I'd say.

It's odd. When you're on the outside and you imagine that, for whatever reason, you might end up spending several years between four walls, you think you wouldn't be able to stand it, that it'd be simply unbearable. And yet, as you see, it is bearable. I, at least, have been able to bear it. I won't deny that I've had moments of despair, desperate moments, made much worse by physical suffering. But I'm talking about pure, unadulterated despair; the kind where you start counting each day as it passes, day after day, and you end up with this one day of being imprisoned, multiplied by many thousands of days. And yet, somehow, the body adapts, better than the mind. The body

I

is first to grow accustomed to the new schedule, new positions, the new rhythm of its needs, its new periods of tiredness and rest, its new activity and non-activity. If you're given a cell-mate, at first you see him as an intruder. But gradually he becomes someone to talk to. This current one is my eighth. I think I've got on pretty well with all of them. What's hard is when the despair you both feel doesn't coincide, and his despair infects you, or your despair infects him. Or sometimes it's the case that one of you just stubbornly refuses to accept the other's despair, refuses the spread of the contagion, and this resistance gives rise to an argument, a bitter stand-off. Then, being cooped up together really doesn't help, it only stirs things up, provokes you (and the other person) to say wounding or sometimes even unforgivable things, which hang in the air, and seem even crueller by the mere fact that you can't avoid the other person's presence. And if things become so tense that the two occupants of that one tiny, confined space won't even exchange a single word, then that awkward, anguished company makes the shared cell much less bearable, much more quickly, than being in complete isolation. Fortunately, in the already lengthy saga of my time here, there has been only one episode of that kind, and it didn't last long. In the end, we both grew so fed up with our silent duet that one evening we looked at one another and started to speak almost in unison. After that it was easy.

It's been almost two months since I had any news from you. I won't ask, because I already know what's going on. And what isn't. They say that in a week everything will be back to normal. I hope so. You've no idea how important a letter is for everyone in here. When we're allowed out into the exercise yard, you can tell straightaway those who've received a letter and those who haven't. The lucky ones' faces are strangely lit up, although they often try to conceal their utter delight to spare the feelings of the less lucky ones. For obvious reasons, in recent weeks all of us have had long faces. And that's no good either. So I have no answers to any of your questions, simply because I don't have any from you. But I do have some questions of my own. Not ones you already know that I'll ask without my having to ask them; ones which, by the way, I don't particularly like to ask just in case you reply (as a joke or, worse, in all seriousness), 'Not any longer.' I wanted to ask you about Dad. He hasn't written to me in ages. And, in his case, I get the impression there's no other reason for my not having heard from him: it's just that he hasn't written to me in a long while. And I can't work out why. Sometimes I go over (in my mind, that is) what I can remember writing in some of my short letters, but I don't think there's anything that could have upset him. Do you see a lot of him these days? And another question: how is Beatriz getting on at school? From the last little letter she wrote, I thought there was something a bit ambiguous about her account. And do you know how much I miss you? Even though I'm pretty good at adapting, that's one of the things neither my mind nor my body can grow accustomed to – being without you. Not so far, that is. Will I ever get used to it? I don't think so. Have you?

Battered and Bruised
(Political actions)

'Graciela,' says the girl, holding a glass in her hand, 'would you like some lemonade?'

She is wearing a white blouse, jeans, sandals. Long, dark hair, but not too long, tied back with a yellow ribbon. Very pale skin. Nine years old, possibly ten.

'I've told you not to call me "Graciela".'

'Why? Isn't that your name?'

'Of course it is. But I would prefer you to call me "Mum", please.'

'All right, but I don't get it. You don't call me "daughter", you say, "Beatriz".'

'That's different.'

'Well, anyway, do you want some lemonade?'

'Yes, thank you.'

Graciela looks somewhere between thirty-two and thirty-five, and possibly even is as old as that. She is wearing a grey skirt and red blouse. Chestnut-coloured hair, and big, expressive eyes. Warm lips, with only a trace of lipstick. She has taken off her glasses to talk to her daughter, but now replaces them so that she can carry on reading.

Beatriz puts the glass of lemonade on a side table that has two ashtrays on it, and leaves the room. Five minutes later, she comes back.

'Yesterday at school I had a fight with Lucila.'

'Ah.'

'You don't want to know why?'

'You're always fighting with Lucila. It must be a way you two have of showing you like each other. Because you're good friends, aren't you?'

'Yes, we are.'

'Well, then?'

'Other times when we fight it's like a game, but yesterday it was serious.'

'Was it?'

'She talked about Dad.'

Graciela takes her glasses off again. Now she is interested. She gulps down the lemonade.

'She said that if Dad is in jail he must be a criminal.'

'And what did you say?'

'I said he wasn't. I said he was a political prisoner. But afterwards I thought I didn't really know what that means. I always hear people say it, but I'm not sure what it is.'

'And that's why you fought?'

'Yes, and also because she said that at home her father says political exiles come here to take local people's jobs.'

'What did you say to that?'

'I didn't know what to say, so I hit her.'

'So now her father will be able to say that the children of political exiles are coming here to beat up his daughter.'

'But I didn't really hit her, it was more of a pat. But she acted like I'd really hurt her.'

Graciela bends forward to straighten a stocking, perhaps also to give herself time to think.

'It was wrong of you to hit her.'

'I guess so. But what was I supposed to do?'

'Well, it's also true that her father shouldn't say things like that. He, of all people, should understand what it's like for us.'

5

'Why *he* of all people?'

'Because he's a man with political ideas.'

'Are you a woman with political ideas?'

Graciela laughs, relaxes slightly. She ruffles her daughter's hair.

'Yes, to some extent, but I've a long way to go.'

'To go where?'

'To be like your father, for example.'

'Is he in jail because of his political ideas?'

'Not exactly. More for his political actions.'

'Do you mean he killed somebody?'

'No, Beatriz, he didn't kill anyone. There are other political actions.'

Beatriz controls herself. She seems to be on the verge of tears, and yet she is smiling.

'Go and fetch me some more lemonade.'

'Yes, Graciela.'

Don Rafael
(Rout and route)

The essential thing is to adapt. I know it's hard at my age. Almost impossible. And yet. After all, my exile is *my* exile. Not everyone has their own. They wanted to impose somebody else's on me. No chance. I made it my own. How? That doesn't really matter. It's neither a secret nor a revelation. I'd say you have to start by taking charge of the streets. The corners. The sky. The cafés. The sun and, most important of all, the shade. It's only when you start to realize that a street isn't strange to you that it stops looking at you like a stranger. It's the same with everything. When I first got here I used a walking stick, as perhaps befits someone aged sixty-seven. But it had nothing to do with my age. It was a sign of how disheartened I was. *Back there* I had always taken the same route home. And that was the thing I missed, being *here*. People don't understand that sort of nostalgia. They think nostalgia has to do only with skies or trees or women. At best, with political activism. The home country, in short. But I have always felt a greyer, less well-defined nostalgia.

That's an example. The route I took back home. It soothes you, gives you peace of mind to know what's coming next, to know what's round every corner, after every streetlamp, every newspaper kiosk. *Here*, on the other hand, when I first set out walking, everything took me by surprise. And all that surprise made me weary. And then, I didn't reach *home*, I just went to *the room.* I was tired of being surprised. Maybe that's why I started using the stick. To stop being thrown off balance. Or perhaps so that any fellow countrymen I met would say: 'But Don Rafael, *back there* you never used a cane,' and I could reply: 'Well, you didn't wear those *guayabera* shirts, either.' Surprises, surprises. One surprise was a shop selling gaudily coloured masks that almost hypnotized me. I couldn't get used to them, even though they were always the same each time I passed by. But always seeing the same masks in the shopfront also led me to wish, or possibly even to expect, that their faces would change, and every day I was astonished to see that they were still the same. That's how the stick helped me. Why? How? Well, I could lean on it every evening when I felt that twinge of disappointment upon dis- covering that the masks still hadn't changed. And I must say that my thinking here wasn't really so absurd. Because a mask is not a face. It's a made object, isn't it? A face is only altered by accident. I mean its structure, not its expression, which is, of course, forever shifting. A mask on the other hand can change for thousands of reasons. For example: as a trial, an experiment, or an adjustment, an improvement, because it's damaged, or replaced. It took me three months to realize there was nothing to be gained from these masks. Those stubborn numbskulls were never going to change. So I started paying attention to faces instead. It turned out to be a good decision. The passing faces were never the same. They came towards me, and I abandoned my stick. I no longer needed it to bear the weight of disillusionment. Each face might stay the same from day to day, but it would change over the years, and those that came towards me (apart from a timid, bony beggar woman) were always new. And with them came all the social classes, some in swanky cars or more modest ones, in buses, wheel- chairs, or simply on foot. I no longer missed the route home in

Montevideo that I knew by heart. In this new city there were new routes to be taken. A new route is not a rout. We were not completely routed, but we did suffer a defeat, we did retreat. I had understood this, but it was only really confirmed to me when I gave my first class here. A student stood up and asked permission to speak. He asked: 'Sir, why did your country, a well-established liberal democracy, turn so quickly into a military dictatorship?' I asked him not to call me 'sir'. We never used to do that. But I said it just to give myself time to construct an answer. I told him what everyone knows: that the process began a long time earlier, in the years of calm, but deep beneath that calm. I put the different headings up on the board, the phases, definitions, corollaries. The youngster nodded. And in his understanding eyes I saw the extent of my rout, of this new route. Ever since, I've taken a different way back in the afternoons. Besides, I no longer return to *a room*. It's not a house either. It's simply an apartment, that is, a pretend house: a room with bits added on. But I like this new city; why wouldn't I? Its inhabitants – thank goodness – have their flaws. And it's great fun for me to detail them. Virtues – of course they have those, too – are usually boring. But not flaws. Kitsch, for example, is such fertile ground here; it never bores me. My stick was an attempt at kitsch, but I had to abandon it. Whenever I feel I'm being kitsch, I despise myself a little, and that's terrible. It's never right to despise yourself unless it's with good reason, which isn't the case for me.

Exiles
(Green horse)

Six months earlier he had slipped on a polished hotel floor, in another city, and hit his head hard on the ground. As a result, one of his retinas had become detached, and now he had been operated on. On medical advice he had to spend a fortnight in bed, with both eyes bandaged, which meant he was completely dependent on his wife. Every seventy-two hours the surgeon came, raised the bandage on his operated eye to make sure everything was fine, and then replaced it. He'd been advised that for the first week at least he should have no visits, so as to get complete rest. But he could listen to the radio and the cassette recorder. And, of course, answer the telephone.

The news bulletins weren't boring, as they had been in the old days; sometimes they were downright terrifying. By January 1975 ten or twelve bodies were being found each day on Buenos Aires rubbish dumps. Between broadcasts he enjoyed listening to cassettes of music by Chico Buarque, Daniel Viglietti, Nacha Guevara, Silvio Rodríguez, but also Schubert's Trout sonata and the occasional Beethoven quartet.

Another distraction was to call up images in his mind. This had become the most fascinating of his passive activities. There was definitely something creative about it, something more original than his eyes' simple, straightforward registering of the images reality presented him. No longer. Now he was the one inventing and summoning that reality, which appeared with all its traits and colours on the inner wall of his closed eyes.

It was a fascinating game. To think, for example: now I'm going to create a green horse in the rain, and then to see it appear on the reverse side of his motionless eyelids. He didn't dare make the horse trot or run, because the doctor had told him his pupils shouldn't move, and with this new discovery he wasn't sure if the affected pupil might be tempted to follow the galloping green horse. But he felt completely free to imagine static paintings. For example: three boys (two blond-haired kids and one little black one, like in the ads for the big American corporations), the first one with a skateboard, the second a cat, the third with a cup and ball. And also, why not, a naked girl, whose vital statistics he carefully chose before completing the image. Or a wide panorama of a Montevideo beach, with one part full of gaily coloured parasols, and another by contrast almost deserted, with a bearded old man in shorts walking a dog that gazed up at its master in an attitude of stiff loyalty . . .

Then the phone rang, and it was easy for him to stretch out his hand. It was a close female friend, who of course knew about the operation but didn't ask how he was getting on or if everything was all right. She also knew that his apartment on Las Heras and Pueyrredón did not give on to the street, but you could get a glimpse of three or four metres of the square from the tiny bathroom window. And yet she said: 'I'm just calling so you'll go out on to the balcony to see the wonderful military parade taking place outside your building.' With that she hung up. So he told his wife to go and take a look out of the bathroom window. It was what he had expected: a military search operation.

'We'll have to burn a few things,' he said, and could imagine the worried look on his wife's face. Despite the urgency of the situation, he did his best to calm her down. 'There's nothing illegal, but if they come in here and find things you can buy at any kiosk, like Che's diaries or the Second Havana Declaration (I'm not talking about Fanon or Gramsci or Lukacs, because they have no idea who they are) or copies of Militancia magazine or the Noticias newspaper, that'll be enough to cause us problems.'

She began to burn books and newspapers, every so often peering out at the corner of the square visible from the bathroom. She had to open other windows (the ones that gave on to the garden between the two blocks) to get rid of the smoke and smell of burning. All this took her twenty minutes. He tried to direct her: 'Look on the second shelf, the fourth and fifth books on the left, they're Aesthetics and Marxism *in two volumes. Can you see them? And on the shelf underneath are* Episodes from the Revolutionary War *and* The State and Revolution.'

She asked him whether she should also burn Socialist Cinema *and* Marx and Picasso. He said she should burn the others first: those two were easier to explain away. 'Don't throw the ashes down the rubbish chute. Try to use the toilet.' The smoke made him cough a little. 'Won't it damage your eyes?' 'Maybe. But we have to choose the lesser evil. Anyway, I don't think it will. They're bandaged tightly.'

The phone rang again. The same friend. 'Well, what do you reckon? Did you enjoy the parade? A shame it was over so quickly, don't you think?' 'Yes,' he said, taking a deep breath, 'it was magnificent. All that discipline, the colours, they looked so elegant. I've been fascinated by military parades ever since I was a kid. Thanks for letting me know.'

'OK, you can stop burning things. For today, at least. They've gone.' His wife also breathed heavily, swept up the last ashes with the brush and pan, tipped them down the toilet, pulled the chain, made sure they were all flushed away. Then she washed her hands and came to sit down, more relaxed, next to the bed. He managed to take hold of one of her hands. 'We can burn the rest tomorrow,' she said, 'but more calmly.'

'It's a shame. They're books I need sometimes.'

He tried to think of the green horse in the rain. For some reason he couldn't fathom, this time the horse was jet-black, and ridden by a stocky rider wearing a military cap who didn't have a face. At least, not one he could make out on the inside walls of his eyelids.

Beatriz

(The seasons)

The seasons are mainly winter, spring and summer. Winter is famous for scarves and snow. When it's winter, old men and women shake and you say that they shiver. I don't shiver because I'm not an old woman, I'm a girl. And also because I always sit near the stove. In books and films winter means that there are sleighs, but we don't have those here. There's no snow either. The winter here is so boring. But there is a wonderful wind that you can feel in the air and all round your ears. Sometimes my Grandpa Rafael says he's going to withdraw into his winter quarters. I don't know why he doesn't withdraw into his summer quarters. It seems to me that if he goes to the winter ones he's going to shiver, because he's quite elderly. You should never say old, you say: elderly. A boy in my class says his grandmother is an old bitch. I taught him that he should at least say she's an elderly bitch.

Another important season is spring. My mum doesn't like spring because that was the season they arested Dad. That's not the same as rested. Without the letter *a* it means sleep. Spelt like that with an *a* it means sort of like going to the police. My dad was arested, and as it was spring he was wearing a green pull-over. Nice things happen in spring, too, like when my friend Arnoldo lends me his skateboard. He would lend it to me in winter as well, but Mum says I'm susceptible and I'll catch a cold. No one else in my class is susceptible. Graciela is my mum. Another great thing about spring is flowers.

But summer is the champion of the seasons because it's sunny and there is no school. In summer the only things that look as if they're shivering are the stars. In summer all human beings sweat. Sweat is something that is sort of like damp. When you sweat in winter it's because you have bronchitis, for example. In summer my forehead sweats. In summer fugitives go to the beach because nobody recognizes them in their swimsuits. At the beach I'm not scared of the fugitives, but I am of dogs and waves. My friend Teresita was not scared of waves, she was very brave and once almost drowned. A man was forced to save her so now she's scared of waves, too, but she's still not scared of dogs.

Graciela, who's my mum, always insists there's a fourth season called thortum. I say that's possible, but I've never seen it. Graciela says that in thortum there is a great abundance of dry leaves. It's always good to have an abundance of something, even if it is in thortum. Thortum is the most mysterious of the seasons because it's neither cold nor hot so you don't know what clothes to wear. That must be why I never know when I'm in thortum. If it's not cold I think it's summer, and if it's not hot I think it's winter. But it turns out to have been thortum. I have winter clothes, summer and spring clothes, but I don't think they'll be any use in thortum. It's thortum now where my dad is, and he wrote that he's very happy because the dry leaves float in through the bars and he imagines they're letters from me.

Intramural

(How are your phantoms doing?)

I spent today staring at the damp patches on the wall. It's a habit I've had since childhood. First I would imagine faces, animals, objects in the patches, then I'd turn them into things that caused me fear, even panic. So it's good, now, to transform the stains into objects or faces and not feel afraid. But it also makes me somehow nostalgic for that distant time when my worst fears were self-inflicted, conjured out of ghostly patches on walls. The adult reasons, or maybe the adult excuses, for the fears we have now are no such phantoms. They are unbearably real. And yet we still sometimes supplement them with phantoms of our own invention, don't you think? By the way, how are your phantoms doing? Make sure they get enough protein, you don't want them to starve to death. A life without phantoms isn't good, a life where all presences are of flesh and blood. But to get back to the damp patches. My cellmate was caught up reading his *Pedro Paramo*, but even so I interrupted him to ask whether he had ever noticed the patch close to the door. 'Not especially, but now you mention it, I can see you're right, there is a patch. What of it?' He looked surprised, but curious. You have to understand that in a place like this, *anything* can be interesting. I can't tell you what it means if all of a sudden we see a bird in between the bars, or (as once happened to me, in a previous cell) a little mouse becomes someone to talk to at the hour of the *angelus*, or the hour of the *demonius*, as Sonia used to joke, remember? So I told my companion I was wondering if he could make out any figure (human, animal or inanimate) in that patch. He stared at it for a while, then said: 'Charles de Gaulle in profile.' Incredible! To me it looked more like an umbrella. When I told him so, he laughed out loud for about ten minutes. That's another good thing when you're in here: being able to laugh. I don't know, but if you really laugh, it's as if your insides have settled down, as if all of a sudden there are reasons to be optimistic, as if all this makes some kind of sense. We ought to prescribe ourselves laughter as therapy. But, as you can imagine, the problem is that there aren't all that many opportunities to laugh. For example, when I realize how long it's been since I last saw you: you, Beatriz, Dad. And, above all, when I think of the time that may pass before I see you again. When I gauge how long that is, well, it's hardly a laughing matter. Then again, it's nothing to cry about. I barely ever cry, actually. But I'm not proud of this emotional constipation of mine. I know a lot of people in here who can just suddenly let it all out and weep inconsolably for half an hour, only to emerge from that pit feeling better, in a better frame of mind. As if the release has helped them adjust. Sometimes I'm sorry I've never acquired the habit. Maybe I'm scared that if I let myself go, the result for me personally wouldn't be better adjustment – it'd be a breakdown. I've always had more than enough screws half-loose to want to risk an even greater collapse. Besides, to be completely frank with you, it's not that I don't cry out of fear of breaking down, but simply because I don't feel like crying; that is, the tears just won't come. That doesn't mean I don't experience anguish, anxiety or other such diversions. It wouldn't be normal if I didn't, given the circumstances. But everyone has their own way of doing things. Mine is to try to overcome these mini-crises through the power of reason. I often succeed. But there are, also, occasions when no amount of reasoning is enough. To misquote that classical author (who was it?) I'd say that sometimes reason *has its hunches* that the heart can't understand. But tell me about you, what you're doing, what you're thinking, what you're feeling. How I'd have loved to walk along the streets you're walking along now, so that we would have something in common there as well. That's the problem with not having travelled much. It's possible that you yourself, but for this unexpected turn of events, would never have visited that city, that country. Maybe, if everything had followed the ordinary course of events – our lives, our marriage, the plans we made no more than seven years ago – we might one day have saved enough to make a long journey (not like the little trips to Buenos Aires, Asunción or Santiago, remember those?), and our destination would probably have been Europe: Paris, Madrid, Rome, London perhaps. How far away all that seems. This upheaval has brought us down to earth, back to our own earth. Now, as you see, if you have to leave, you go to another country here in the Americas. It's only logical. And even those who now, for whatever reason, are in Stockholm, Paris, Brescia or Amsterdam or Barcelona, even they would no doubt wish they were in one of the cities on our continent. After all, I, too, have left our country, in a sense. I yearn for what you yearn for. Exile (internal or external) is bound to be a key word for this decade – you know, someone will probably strike out this sentence. But whoever does so needs to remember that he, too, in some strange way, is also an exile from our real country. If the sentence has survived, you'll have seen how understanding I've become. I amaze myself sometimes. It's life, my girl, life. If it didn't get through, no worries. It wasn't important. Kisses and more kisses for you, from me.

The Other
(Solitary witness)

Shit, what bags under my eyes, Rolando Asuero said to himself in front of the mirror. Confronting the mirror and his hangover. Serves me right for drinking so much, he added, trying to make his eyes look as big as possible, but only managing to appear like a lunatic. Lunang-utan. He pronounced it slowly, and had to smile, despite his thumping headache. That's what Silvio used to call the military back *in illo tempore* when he and his friends would meet up in the cabin at the Solís resort, just before the future began to look so unhealthy. They're not even gorillas, he would declare. Just about orang-utans. And they're lunatics. In other words: lunang-utans.

The four of them: Silvio, Manolo, Santiago and he had got together for what turned out to their be last holiday together. The women were there, too, or rather, the wives. Only three of them, in fact: María del Carmen, Tita and Graciela, because he, Rolando Asuero, was a confirmed bachelor and never wanted to get his occasional flings mixed up with his friends' all-too-stable relationships. But the wives always talked gossip and fashion and horoscopes and recipes, at least back then, and maybe that was why the four men hunkered down on their own to put the world to rights. And they almost succeeded. Silvio, for example, was a really good guy, if a bit naive. He always swore he'd never be able to use a shooter, and yet later on he did, and they certainly used them on him, which is why now he's in Buceo cemetery, more precisely in his in-laws' family crypt, who are still wealthy even if they're sad about it all. And plump María del Carmen far away in Barcelona with her two kids, selling pots on the Ramblas or wherever they are holed up now. Manolo was caustic, sharp and sarcastic, three words that mean almost the same thing but in him were not exactly synonymous. They were more like trenches he had dug to conceal his shyness. The proof of this was that he never went too far, and in the end, he was always gentle and understanding. 'Titfer, bandana, rope sandals / endlessly gazing.' Apart from the titfer, that tango could have been describing him. Santiago, of course, was Mister Know-All, but he was a good sort. He knew about botany and Marxism and stamp-collecting and avant-garde poetry, and he was a living encyclopaedia of the history of football. And not just the goal by Peindibeni against the divine Zamora, or the 'It's yours, Hector!' when we won the World Cup. Those had already become popular legend. Santiago also had the complete file stowed away in his mind, game by game, of the Nazassi Domingos duo (he was a supporter of Nacional through and through) or Perucho Petrone's last season, when out of every ten shots he had on goal eight went straight up in the air, but by some miracle the other two hit the back of the net; and also, to show he had no favourites, he admitted that Skinny Schiaffino was a genius even without the ball, which is the hardest thing to do in a team, and spoke of the respect he had always felt for a mountain of a man called Obdulio, who took no nonsense from anybody, not even Monkey Gambetta.

And now, shit, just look at those bags under my eyes, Rolando Asuero says out loud to himself as he gazes into the rusty mirror: 'I grew up knowing sorrow, and drank my youth away.' While it was true he had known sorrow, he had been drinking other things. Here's the mystery he puzzles over. Why is it that, every so often, let's say once a month, he'll go out on a bender, whereas between sprees he stays sober, almost abstemious? Almost, because there's the occasional *clarete* (or *rosé*, as those who've suffered from Cartesian cultural penetration like to call it) and, well, *clarete* is like communion wine with testosterone. It must be that homesickness comes on with the moon, like women's menstrual cycles. Not just women, but also the eleven thousand virgins and the holy mother, of whom there's only one, well that seems a bit out of proportion, doesn't it? Anyway, better to be a well-known drunk than an anonymous alcoholic. Who can have thought that one up? The fact is, Alcoholics Anonymous always got his goat. You got drunk, or you didn't, according to your own desires or depression or needs or homesickness or rage, and not according to the dictates of the Immaculate or of coercive Puritans. What a great goddam con trick Puritanism is, thinks Rolando Asuero, pulling a face. And he pauses as he considers the fine example north of the Rio Grande. Another great con trick. A moral campaign against the daily evening martini or bourbon, but hurrah for the daily morning napalm.

Ah, if only he could blame imperialism for the bags under his eyes. No chance. 'Lone witness, the oil lamp's light.' He doesn't need individual or group therapy. Everyone knows how hard exile can be. Even that poor psychoanalyst had a tough time. Back there, he refused to hand over the records of his subversive patients, and still less of his impatient subversives. Of course he had a tough time. The cops dole out their own brand of therapy, they don't want competitors. *Lone witness.* Silvio dead, Manolo in Gothenburg, Santiago in Montevideo Prison. And María del Carmen, widowed by the repression, selling her bits of pottery. And Tita, separated from Manolo and now living with a really serious kid (I'm going to *accompanion* myself with Sardine Estévez, she had written a year earlier), in Lisbon, no less. And Graciela, here, thrown off balance, and beautiful, with Santiago's little Beatriz, slaving away as a secretary. And him? Shit, look at those bags under his eyes.

In this blessed and cursed country, the people really are great. Why deny it? He likes their broad smiles, especially on the women's faces. But there are days and there are nights when he doesn't like them so much. Those are the days and nights when he misses what's implicit, the shared assumptions, all the things that don't need to be said . . . Days and nights when he has to explain everything and listen to everything. One of the modest pleasures of making love to someone from your own country is that if at some point (in that zero hour that always follows the urgency, the enthusiasm, the give and take, up and down) you don't feel like talking, you can say or hear just a brief monosyllable, and that little word becomes charged with associations, implied meanings, shared symbols, a common past, who knows what else? There's nothing to explain or be explained. There's no need to pour your heart out. Your hands can do the talking: they're wordless, but they can be extremely eloquent. Boy, can they be eloquent. Monosyllables, as well, but only when they bring with them their whole train of associations, implications. Amazing how many languages can fit into a single one, Rolando Asuero says and tells himself, contemplating his own reflection. Then he repeats, gloomily: Shit, those bags!

Exiles
(Cordially invited)

At approximately six p.m. on Friday 22 August 1975, I was reading, relatively carefree, in the apartment I rented on Calle Shell in the Miraflores district of Lima, when someone rang the bell downstairs and asked for Señor Mario Orlando Benedetti. That already smelt fishy because my middle name only appears in official documents. None of my friends ever uses it.

I went down and a man in plain clothes showed me his ID: Peruvian Investigative Police. He said he had a few questions he wanted to ask me concerning my papers. We went upstairs and he told me they had been informed that my visa had expired. I brought my passport and showed him the visa had been renewed in time. 'You're going to have to come with me anyway, because the boss wants a word with you. You'll be back within half an hour,' he assured me. This desultory promise all but convinced me I was going to be deported. It was the kind of cryptic language favoured by repressive forces the world over.

During the short journey to police headquarters, he passed the time criticizing the government. He was setting clumsy traps, too naively, luring me to take the bait and join in with his criticism of the Peruvian Revolution. My praise was cagey but precise.

After we reached police headquarters, I was made to wait half an hour, and then I was seen by an inspector. He repeated the story of my expired visa, and I once again showed my passport. Then he said I was doing paid work, which was prohibited on a tourist visa. I told him mine was a special case, because, with the explicit authorization of the

Ministry of Foreign Affairs, the Expreso newspaper had signed a con-tract for me to work as a journalist, and this contract was at that very moment sitting at the highest level in the Ministry of Labour. The inspector was a bit taken aback by this 'at the highest level' until another official, doubtless his superior, shouted from a nearby desk: 'Don't give him any more explanations! He'll only come back with more of the same. Get to the point!' Then he turned to me: 'The Peruvian govern-ment wants you out of here.' And in response to the logical question, 'Might I know why?': 'No. We don't know why either. The minister sends the order and we carry it out.' 'How long do I have?' 'If possible, ten minutes. But since that's not going to happen, there's no way you can get out that quickly, let's say you must leave at the soonest feasible moment: in an hour or two.' 'Can I choose where I go?' 'Where do you want to go? Bear in mind we're not paying your fare.' 'Well, seeing that in Argentina I've had death threats from the AAA,* and since I once worked in Cuba for two years and have the possibility of finding employment there again, I'd like to know if I'm allowed to go to Cuba.' 'No. There's no plane leaving for Cuba today, and you have to leave as soon as possible.' 'All right, then tell me what my options actually are.' 'They are: either we take you by road and leave you on the border with Ecuador, or you use your return ticket to Buenos Aires.'

I quickly thought it through. The idea of a military truck dumping me at first light on the border of a country I didn't know was not exactly appealing, so I said: 'Buenos Aires. I've never been to Ecua-dor.' I had to sign a statement in which I was asked how I received my fees from Expreso. I said, from the Central Bank, and once again pointed out that I had a contract that was duly authorized by the Ministry of Labour, etc.

We returned to the apartment. At first, they gave me a quarter of an hour to pack, then a whole hour. They made phone calls, but could

---

* AAA: The Argentine Anti-Communist Alliance was a far-right paramilitary group who kidnapped and murdered people in Argentina in the early 1970s.

not find me a seat on any flight to Buenos Aires, which gave me some more time. But they would only allow me to take one suitcase, so I had to leave lots of things behind.

The inspector then told me (by now they were treating me more amicably) that mine wasn't a case of expulsion or deportation, and that therefore they would not stamp 'Deported' on my passport. Deportation – he explained – required an executive decree, and, in my case, none had been issued. Which meant that this was simply 'a cordial invitation to leave the country at once'. I asked what would happen if I declined the invitation. 'Ah, but then you'd be leaving all the same.' I told him that, in my country, when faced with a choice of that sort, we used to say, 'That doesn't make a shitload of difference.'

I asked if I could make a call to someone in Lima. They didn't allow that: I was to be held incommunicado. On the other hand, they did let me make a few long-distance calls. So I rang my brother in Montevideo, and asked him to tell my wife to come and meet me in Buenos Aires. I also tried to ring two or three people in Buenos Aires, but couldn't get through. I wanted to make sure there would be somebody there to receive me when I reached Ezeiza Airport. I asked them to at least let me speak to my landlady. They told me I could, as long as I told her that I had suddenly decided to leave Peru and was therefore quitting the apartment at once. I said I wouldn't make any such call, as she had always been very decent in her dealings with me. I suggested they ring her instead. They refused.

After a few minutes the inspector asked me on what conditions would I talk to the landlady; I said I'd like to speak to her if I could tell her I was being thrown out of the country. He eventually accepted and so, at three in the morning, I called her. The poor woman nearly fainted. 'Oh, señor, why would they do something like that to a gentleman like you!' I explained that I'd leave an inventory of the things of mine that were still in the apartment, and would let her know later on where they should be sent.

By now, the four men were so relaxed that one even asked me for a poster with one of my songs that was up on the wall, and another asked for one of my books. 'Aren't you worried it might compromise you?' I asked. 'Let's hope not,' he said, not entirely convinced.

Since the night had grown pretty cold by then, two of the men asked their boss for permission to go and fetch jumpers. He agreed. I went on packing under the watchful eye of the other two. All of a sudden, I noticed they had both fallen asleep. They were snoring so peacefully that I took off my shoes so my footsteps on the floor wouldn't disturb them. That gave me another hour and a half to sort my case out properly, during which time the rubbish chute was kept quite busy.

At the end of the hour and a half, I put my shoes back on and gently shook the inspector: 'Sorry to wake you, but if I'm so subversive that you're throwing me out of the country, please at least stay awake and keep an eye on me.' The inspector explained the problem was that they had been working since early that morning and were exhausted. I said I understood, but that wasn't my fault.

At half-past four, the five of us left (by then, the other two had returned with their sweaters) in a big black car. We stopped off at the landlady's house. They gave her the keys and the inventory. That drive was my only real cause for concern, because they took me along an unusual route. Completely dark, through a wasteland lit only by our car's headlights. It took much longer than the normal way to the airport. When I finally caught sight of the control tower lights in the distance, I confess I breathed a little easier. At the airport, the soonest I could leave was on the nine o'clock Saturday evening flight. Fortunately, it was on an AeroPeru aeroplane. They hadn't managed to get me a seat on the eight o'clock one with LAN Chile.

At no point did they give me anything to drink or eat. I went twenty-four hours without tasting a thing. I think this was simply due to the fact that they had no money: they didn't eat anything either. When the inspector handed me my documents at the foot of the aircraft steps, he said: 'I'm sure you're leaving feeling pretty sore towards the Peruvian government, but don't hold it against Peruvians.' And he shook my hand.

Battered and Bruised
(A landscape or two)

Graciela went into the bedroom, slipped off her light raincoat, looked at herself in the dressing-table mirror, and frowned. Then she removed her blouse and skirt, and collapsed on the bed. She raised her leg, stretched it out as far as she could. She noticed a ladder in her stocking. Sitting up, she took both nylons off and looked to see if there were any more holes in them. She folded them into a little pile and put them on a chair. She looked at herself in the mirror once again, and pressed her fingers to her temples.

The fading light of what had been a cool, blustery afternoon filtered in through the window. She pulled back one of the lace curtains and peered out. Six or seven children were playing outside Block B. She recognized Beatriz, hair unkempt and out of breath, but obviously enjoying herself. Smiling wanly, Graciela ran her fingers through her own hair.

The telephone rang on the bedside table. Rolando. She lay back down to speak more comfortably.

'What a crap afternoon, isn't it?' he said.

'It's not that bad. I like the wind. I don't know why, but when I walk into it, it blows things away. I mean, the things I want blown away.'

'Such as?'

'Don't you read the papers? Don't you know that's called intervention in the internal affairs of another nation?'

'Whatever you say, Ms Republic.'

'A friendly republic, I hope.'

She transferred the receiver to the left side so that she could scratch behind her other ear.

'Any news?' he asked.

'A letter from Santiago.'

'That's great.'

'It's a bit puzzling.'

'In what way?'

'He talks about damp patches on the walls and the shapes he used to imagine he saw in them as a boy.'

'That happened to me, too.'

'It happens to everyone, doesn't it?'

'Well, it may not be hugely original, but I don't see why it's so puzzling. Or did you want him to write a polemic against the military?'

'Don't be silly. It's just that I think he used to be more confident, take more risks.'

'Yes, sure. And perhaps that's why you had to go for a month without hearing from him.'

'I've already checked. It was a measure taken out against all of them. One of the many collective punishments . . .'

'Collective punishments that are, generally, based on such puerile pretexts as: the writing of a letter which, deliberately or otherwise, oversteps a mark that has never been formally established, but which is, nonetheless, very much in place.'

She didn't reply. A few seconds later Rolando spoke again:

'How is Beatriz?'

'She's outside, playing with her gang.'

'I've got a soft spot for that girl. She's so healthy and full of life.'

'Yes. Much more than me.'

'Well, that's not really so. It's true she gets most of her energy from Santiago, but it comes from you, as well.'

27

'I can see it coming from Santiago.'

'From you as well. It's just that you've been a little depressed recently.'

'Possibly. The problem is, I just can't see any way out. And besides, my work bores me stiff.'

'You will find something more stimulating. For now, though, you've got to put up with it.'

'Now you're supposed to say how lucky I've been.'

'You've been lucky.'

'You're also supposed to tell me that not all exiles from the far south have found a well-paid job for only six hours a day, and with Saturdays off, too.'

'Not all exiles from the far south have found such a well-paid job, etcetera. Can I add that you're such an efficient secretary, you deserve it?'

'You can. But that efficiency is precisely why I'm so bored. It would be more interesting if I made a mistake occasionally.'

'I don't think so. You might get bored of being so efficient, but in general bosses and managers get much more bored, much sooner, with inefficiency.'

Again, she said nothing. And again, he was the one to take up the conversation.

'Can I make you a proposition?'

'So long as it's not dishonest.'

'Let's say it's semi-honest.'

'Then I'll only half-accept it. What is it?'

'Would you like to go to the movies?'

'No, Rolando.'

'It's a good film.'

'I don't doubt it. I trust your taste. At least, your taste in films.'

'It'll blow your cobwebs away a little.'

'I'm happy with my cobwebs.'

'That's worse still. So, I'll repeat the invitation: do you want to go to the movies?'

'No, Rolando. Thank you, really, but I'm exhausted. If I didn't have to cook something for Beatriz, I swear I'd go to bed without eating.'

'That's no good either. Anything is better than getting worn down by routine.'

Graciela cradled the receiver between her chin and shoulder, her skill as a professional secretary on show. Now her hands were free, allowing her to study her fingernails and file them with an emery board.

'Rolando.'

'Yes, still here.'

'Have you ever been on a train, sitting by the window, across from another person?'

'I think so, though I can't remember when, exactly. Why do you ask?'

'Have you ever noticed that if the two people start talking about the scenery they're watching pass by, the way it's described by the person facing forwards isn't exactly the same as it is by the one facing backwards?'

'I have to confess I've never noticed that. But I'm sure you're right.'

'Well, I've always noticed it. Ever since I was a little girl, whenever I travelled by train I loved looking out at the scenery. It was one of my favourite pastimes. I never read on train journeys. Even now when I'm on a train, I don't like to read. I'm completely drawn in by the countryside flying by. And when I'm facing forward, I feel as if the scenery is rushing towards me and, I don't know, it makes me feel optimistic.'

'What if you're facing backwards?'

'I feel as if the scenery is pulling away from me, dwindling, dying. Frankly, it depresses me.'

'Which way are you facing now?'

'Don't make fun of me. I remembered all this, really clearly, the other day when I started rereading Santiago's letters. Even though he's in prison, he writes as if life were rushing up to him, coming towards him. But for me, even if I am what you might call free, it's like the scenery is dwindling, dying, running out.'

'That's not bad. As a bit of poetry, that is.'

'It's not poetry. It's not even prose. It's just how I feel.'

'All right, now I'm being serious. I'm worried about your state of mind, you know that? And although I'm convinced that we can each only solve our own problems, it's also true that at times someone we really trust can do something to help – if nothing more than that. And I'm offering you a little bit of help, if you want it. But the main thing is for you to open up, to dig deeper inside yourself.'

'Dig deeper inside myself? You might be right. Maybe. But I'm not certain I'll like what's underneath.'

Don Rafael
(A strange guilt)

Santiago has complained to Graciela that I haven't written to him in ages. And it's true. What was I supposed to say? That what he's going through is the result of his attitude? He already knows that. Was I supposed to tell him that I feel a bit guilty for not having talked with him enough (back when it was still time to talk, and not to swallow your words) and convinced him not to go down that road? Perhaps he doesn't know for definite that I feel guilty, but he probably suspects as much – and suspects that, had we had those serious discussions, he would have continued down the road he had chosen for himself, regardless. Should I write that whenever I wake up at night I can't shake off the fear, the sense, or the foreboding, or whatever it is, that possibly, at that very moment, he is being tortured, or is recovering from the last torture session, or steeling himself for the next one, or screaming curses at someone? Maybe he doesn't want to contemplate anything like that. He must have more than enough to do, dealing with his own suffering, isolation, his own anguish. When you're suffering, you have no need to add the burden of other people's pain to your own. But sometimes I imagine that they're holding the cattle prod against Santiago's testicles and at that same instant I feel a real (not imaginary) pain tear through *my own* testicles. Or if I imagine they're waterboarding him I feel as if I'm literally drowning, too. Why? It's an old story, or rather, an old warning sign: the survivor of genocide feels a strange guilt simply because he is still alive. And the person who, for whatever perfectly good reason (I'm not counting the ignoble ones) has managed to escape torture, still feels guilt for not being tortured. So in other words, I've not got much to write to him about. Obviously, there are certain topics that can't be mentioned in a letter to a prisoner, especially one thrown in jail for being a subversive. And yet there are other things I could write, but I'm the one choosing to censor them, to leave them out. And the things left to write about after these two restrictions are imposed are all pretty inane. Would Santiago want me to write stupidities? There is one thing that, were the circumstances different, I would write to him, or better still talk to him about, but never in the current situation. By which I mean Graciela's state of mind. Graciela is not well. She's becoming increasingly dispirited, greyer. In the past she was always so pretty, so lively, so sharp. The worst of it is, I think I've worked out that her despondency is due to her drifting away from Santiago. The reasons? How can one know? I'm sure she thinks highly of him. She isn't at odds with him over his politics, because she is (or was) of the same mind. Can it be that, to keep her love intact, a woman needs a man's physical presence, more beyond the mere knowledge that he exists? Can it be that Ulysses is becoming domesticated, while Penelope is no longer content to weave and unpick? Who knows. The fact is, if I can't bring myself to mention it to her, when I see her almost every day, how could I possibly mention it to Santiago, to whom I only send a letter every once in a while? I could also tell him about my classes, and the questions the students ask. Or perhaps about an idea I have, about getting back to writing. Another novel? No, one failure is enough. Possibly a book of short stories. Not for publication. At my age that's not so important.

I sense it would be a stimulus for me. I haven't written a word in fifteen years. At least, nothing literary. And, for fifteen years, I've had no desire to do so. But now, suddenly, I do. Could this be a sign? Something I need to interpret? A symptom? But of what?

Intramural
(The river)

I've come from the river. Do you think I'm deranged? Not in the least. If I didn't go mad in other circumstances, I reckon I'm inoculated against insanity by now. And yet I come from the river. I discovered the trick a few weeks ago. Before that, memories assailed me at random. All of a sudden, I would be thinking of you or Dad, then two seconds later it'd be a book I read when I was in high school, then almost immediately the puddings the old lady used to make me when we lived on Hocquart Street. In other words, I was being tyrannized by my memories. Then one evening, I thought, I'm going to free myself from this tyranny. And from that moment on, I've been the one controlling my memories. Not completely, of course. There are always moments during the day (generally when I feel low or depressed) when they overwhelm me. But that's not usually the case. What usually happens is: I plan my memory, that is, I take charge and choose what I'm going to remember. So I decide to recall, for example, a far-off day at primary school, or a night out with friends, or one of the interminable debates in the Union of Uruguayan University Students, or the swaying details (to the extent that those can, in fact, be remembered) of some of my rare boozy sprees, or a serious discussion with Dad, or the morning Beatriz was born. Of course I alternate all this with my memories of you, but I've decided to put those into some kind of order as well. Because if

I don't, then all those images are focused on your body, on you and me making love. And that's not always good for me. It becomes a painful reminder of your absence. Or of my absence. To start with, I feel an anguished mental pleasure. I enjoy myself in a vacuum. Then I grow depressed. And my depression lasts for hours. So, when I say that here, too, I had to put things in order, I mean I've decided to incorporate other memories of you (and me) that are as important and cherished as the nights our bodies spent together. We've had so many conversations that for me, at least, were unforgettable. Do you remember the Saturday when I convinced you – after five dialectical hours – of the new path we had to take? And when we were in Mendoza? And Asunción? The dates don't matter. What's important is the order I impose, the way I recall them. That's why I began by saying that today I've come from the river. That's a memory that doesn't involve you. It was the Río Negro, near Mercedes. When I was eleven or twelve, I used to spend the holidays at my aunt and uncle's place. Their property wasn't particularly big (in fact, it was little more than a small farm), but it did lead down to the river. Because there were lots of leafy trees between the house and the water, when I was on the riverbank no one could see me. And I loved that solitude. It was one of the rare occasions I heard, saw, smelt, touched and tasted nature. The birds would come close; they weren't scared off by my presence. Maybe they thought I was a little tree or bush. Usually, there was a gentle breeze, and maybe that was why the trees didn't argue, didn't tussle among themselves; they simply exchanged opinions, nodded good-humouredly, waved me their support. Sometimes I leant back against one or other of the most ancient among them, and the rough bark conveyed an almost paternal understanding. To feel the bark of an age-old tree is like stroking the mane of a horse you ride every day. You commune with it in a quiet, understated way (not like the cloying relationship with an unbearably faithful dog), but it's intense enough that you miss it when you return to the bustle of the city. On other days I would climb into the boat and row out to the middle of the river. Being halfway between the two banks was particularly exciting. Above all, because they were so utterly divided, so at odds with one another. This wasn't so much marked by the birds, who flew from bank to bank, but more by the trees, which seemed to regard themselves as local and partisan, set firmly in their own worlds, in other words, on their own shores. I did nothing. I simply stayed and observed. I didn't read or play. Life flowed over me, from shore to shore. I felt part of that life, and came to the strange conclusion that it must not be boring to be a pine, a weeping willow or eucalyptus. But, as I learned a few years later, keeping an equal distance can never last for long, and eventually I had to decide on one shore or the other. And it was clear I belonged to only one of them. So you can see how it's true, what I said to you at the beginning: I've come from the river.

Beatriz
(Skyscrapers)

The singular is written skyscraper and in the plural it's sky-scrapers. The same with toothpick: you don't say teethpicks. Skyscrapers are buildings with loads of bathrooms. The great advantage of this is that thousands of people can wee at the same time. Skyscrapers also have other advantages. For example, they have lifts that make your tummy feel funny. Lifts that make your tummy feel funny are very modern. Extremely elderly buildings don't have lifts or they only have lifts that don't do anything to your tummy and the people who live or work there die of shame because they are very retarded.

Graciela, in other words my mum, works in a skyscraper. Once she took me to her office and that was the only time I weed in a skyscraper. It's brilliant. Graciela's skyscraper has a funny tummy lift that is completely imported and so it makes my tummy tumble a lot. The other day I told the story in class and all the children were jealous and wanted me to take them to the lift in Graciela's skyscraper. But I told them it was very dangerous because it goes so quickly and if you stick your head out of the window it can be chopped off. And they believed me, the silly-billies. As if lifts in skyscrapers were so retarded as to have windows.

When there's a power cut in skyscraper lifts, panic abounds. In my class when it's break-time, joy abounds. The word 'abounds' is a lovely word.

As well as dizzy lifts, skyscrapers have doormen. Doormen are fat and could never climb the stairs. When doormen lose weight they're not allowed to work in skyscrapers any more, but they have the possibility of being taxi-drivers or football players.

Skyscrapers are divided into tall ones and low ones. Low skyscrapers have many fewer toilets than the tall ones. Low skyscrapers are called houses, but they're forbidden to have gardens. Tall skyscrapers make a lot of shade, but it's different to the shade from trees. I prefer the shade from trees, because it has patches of sunlight and also it moves around. In the shade from tall skyscrapers, serious faces and people begging abound. In the shade from trees, grass and ladybirds abound.

I think that where my dad is when night falls it must be sadness that abounds. I'd really like it for my dad to be able for example to visit the skyscraper where Graciela, that is my mum, works.

Exiles
(He came from Australia)

I met him at Mexico City Airport, by the Cubana de Aviación check-in desk. I was travelling to Havana with three suitcases and had to pay the excess. A man behind me in the queue suggested that, since he had only one small case, we should register our luggage together: they came to exactly the permitted 40 kilos. Obviously, I accepted, and thanked him. The Cubana employee despatched the four suitcases. It so happened that when my spontaneous benefactor showed his passport, to my surprise I saw that it was a Uruguayan document. Not an official or diplomatic passport, that is, an ordinary one. He smiled. 'You find this odd, no?' I admitted that I did. 'I'll explain. Let's have a coffee.'

We had our coffee. He asked: 'You're Benedetti, aren't you?' 'Yes, I am. But where do you know me from? I don't remember your face.' 'That's not surprising. You were up on a platform and I was a face in the crowd. I heard you many times in the hustings for the 1971 election campaign. Do you recall the final meeting of the Frente Amplio,* outside the parliament, when the Diagonal Agraciada was completely packed? You didn't speak on that occasion, but you were up on the platform. The General† was very good.'

I think he was offering up these details so that I would trust him,

---

* Frente Amplio: The coalition of left-wing parties in Uruguay in the early 1970s.
† General Liber Seregni, one of the founders of the Frente Amplio. He was imprisoned from 1973 to 1984.

but by that point he needn't have bothered. He had the face of an honest man; he was hiding nothing. He told me his name. It was different, but here I'll call him Falco. His real surname is just as Uruguayan. 'To start with, I should say I've been living in Australia for about five years now. I'm a workman over there. A plumber.' 'And why are you going to Cuba?' 'As a tourist. Part of a group. I've been saving up for two years to go there for a week. It's been my dream.' 'How are you getting on in Australia?' 'As far as money goes, it's fine. But that's all. What's more, as you'll know, che *–' he switched to the less formal mode of address – 'the emigration to Australia wasn't exactly political, it was more economic, although you might say that that means it was indirectly political. Which is true, even if, as a rule, economic migrants aren't really aware of the link. In that sense it's pretty tough, and very different to exile in other places. Sometimes you get a break, like when the Olimareños come and people go to listen to them because, in spite of everything, we're still moved by tunes from our homeland. And it's not just the songs. It's the mention of names of trees, flowers, hills, figures from our history, the streets, towns, references to the sky, the sunsets, the rivers, to every tiny little creek. But the Olimas leave and we all fall back into our routine and our isolation. I always say that, in Australia, we are the Uruguayan Archipelago, because in fact we make up a series of islands, islets, single guys or couples or families, all isolated from each other, existing in solitude, comfortable perhaps, but in solitude nonetheless. Some send money to their families back in Uruguay. That gives their lives and work some meaning, at least.' 'Do they not try to integrate, to make Australian friends?' 'Look, it's not easy. First there's the language barrier. Obviously, over time anyone can end up learning good English, but by then you've already got used to living in isolation, and it's hard to change your habits. Besides, even if they are in need of foreign labour, Australian society doesn't readily open itself up to immigrants. I've gone into a lot of Australian homes, but only as a plumber. If the family's there together when I go past with my toolbox,* they automatically stop talking.' 'And why were you so interested in going to Cuba?' 'I don't know exactly. It's just a kind of fantasy I have, the way you do when you're a child or a teenager. You'll say that a dumb guy like me is too old for fantasies, but it's a real fixation, you know? God, I just said "fixation", it must be a good five years since I've used that word. In Australia you don't just lose your vocabulary, but also, without realizing it, you start incorporating English words into your daily speech. Well, getting back to Cuba: the truth is, we set our sights way too high in Uruguay back in '69 and '70 and a little less so in 1971. We thought radical change was possible in our country as well. But it wasn't, at least, it won't be for a long, long while. So I've been anxious to get to know a place like Cuba which has really been able to bring about change. Tell me, d'you think there'll be any chance of me staying on in Cuba? Working, of course.' 'Wait and see how you feel there. Think, for example, that you might like the people, you may agree with the political system and yet you might be crushed by the climate. Forget the four seasons, in Cuba there's only summer, with a dry period and a rainy one. It doesn't have much effect on me person-ally, but I know other people from the River Plate region who just get exhausted by that unrelenting heat and humidity. Anyway, seven days isn't enough time to get through all the paperwork. Remem-ber there's a weekend in the middle.' 'Yes, I know, but I mean, do Cubans welcome foreigners?' 'You wouldn't be a foreigner there. You're Latin American, aren't you? The issue is more complicated than that. Think for a moment what would happen if Cuba, which has opened its doors so that all those who aren't happy there now can leave, opened those same doors to everybody who wanted to come and live there? Imagine the queues that would form in Montevideo, Buenos Aires, Santiago, La Paz, Port-au-Prince! In any case, there are still huge problems with housing.' 'But do you think I should try?' 'Sure, give it a try. You've nothing to lose.'

That soft, anonymous but familiar voice which in every airport in the world informs passengers to start boarding for their flight instructed us to head for Gate Eight. We carried on talking throughout the flight and when the stewardess (in Cubana de Aviación, they call them flight attendants) passed us our snacks, Falco remarked: 'Wow, incredible. They're not Barbie dolls, like on other airlines. They're real women, did you see?'

In Havana, I lost him at the José Martí Airport after we had collected our suitcases (one of his, three of mine). He headed off to join the rest of his group, and I met several friends who had come to welcome me.

Two days later, there was a march past the North American Interests Office. The invasion of the Peruvian Embassy by 10,000 Cubans* was already over. Now there was a different story: naval manoeuvres had been announced at the Guantanamo base and Carter was making daily threats.

I joined in the march along the Malecón with my colleagues from the Casa de las Américas publishing house. In all the years I had been a resident in Cuba, I had never seen such an impressive demonstration. We were waiting on La Rampa for the march to begin, when all of a sudden I saw Falco some ten metres away from me.

The crowd was so dense it was hard to move, so I shouted to him: 'Falco! Falco!' He heard me straightaway, but must have thought it was impossible that forty-eight hours after arriving in Havana someone had recognized him and was calling out his name. But that's chance for you: I must have been the only person in Cuba who could have recognized him, and there I was, only a few steps away.

Finally, he saw me and looked astonished. He raised his long arms enthusiastically. It took ten minutes for us to reach one another. He gave me a hug. 'How amazing, che! A million people and you've found me!' He was euphoric. 'This does me a power of good. Doesn't

* In April 1980, thousands of Cubans stormed the Peruvian Embassy in Havana, seeking asylum in order to leave the island. This became the Mariel exodus, when as many as 125,000 Cubans were allowed to travel to Miami.

it remind you of the last Frente Amplio meeting?' 'Well, there's more of us here.' 'Of course. But I mean the fervour, the joy.'

At last we set off, at first slowly, then a little faster. All at once I felt him nudge me meaningfully with his elbow. 'D'you know, today I took the first step?' 'What first step?' 'To stay here.' 'Ah.' 'I went to an office someone told me about. It was where lots of people who want to leave, the ones they call "worms", go to obtain permission. I reached the glass door just as they were closing it. I started waving at the employee inside. He shook his head. I insisted he should listen to me, if only for a moment. Then an idea struck me. I had a piece of paper in my pocket. I wrote the word "Comrade" on it and held it up against the glass. Perhaps curiosity got the better of him, because he opened the door about five centimetres, just enough for us to be able to hear one another. "We're not accepting any more requests to leave today, got it?" "I know, but that's not why I'm here." "So why did you come?" "I'm with a group. Tourists. And I want to stay here." "To do what?" "To. Stay. Here." The lad (because he was no more than a lad) couldn't believe his ears. He opened the door a little further so that I could enter. That led, understandably, to protests from the candidates for exile in Miami. "Did you say you wanted to stay?" "Yes, that's what I said." The lad stared at me, as if examining me closely. Then he picked up a notebook, tore out a sheet, wrote a name on it and handed it to me. "Look, man, come back tomorrow, but make it very early. Ask for this comrade. He'll take care of you. And good luck." So tomorrow I'm going there. What d'you reckon? Or as they say here, what do you opine?' 'I see you're picking up Cuban lingo faster than Australian.' The march gathered speed. Gradually we were separated, and for a while I lost sight of him. It was when we were right outside the North American Interests Office (no one was visible at the windows) that I saw him once more. By then he was a little way behind me. In a loud voice with a strong Montevidean accent, he was shouting one of the slogans the good-natured crowd was chanting: 'One-two-three, worms into the sea!'

The Other

(To want to, be able to, etc.)

You're nuts, Rolando Asuero clearly recalls Silvio muttering,
the morning Manolo set out what he termed 'A Personal and
Panoramic Vision of National Reality and Other Essays'. But
Manolo, who by then had been talking only for half an hour at
most, pursed his lips and said, Let me finish, will you? And Silvio had let him finish. Now tell me what you think, Manolo
said smugly, when he finally reached his conclusion. You're
nuts! Silvio had obstinately insisted, and they almost came to
blows. But Santiago and he, Rolando, had stepped in quickly,
and besides María del Carmen and Tita were already close to
tears from sheer nervousness: not Graciela, though, because
she was always tougher – or more stable, or more reserved. So
Silvio and Manolo sat down again. Silvio began to take it out
on the *maté*,* sucking on the metal straw so loudly it could be
heard three dunes away. The fact is, Manolo's thesis did seem
very accurate, but also very alarmist. Circular, Silvio declared,
and yes, it was circular and offered no way out, but Manolo
gave it an emphasis that made it convincing. Those who had
the money and power would never give way. Don't fool

---

* *maté*: This drink is typical of Uruguay and Argentina, a kind of bitter
herbal tea which is served in a gourd and drunk through a metal straw.
There is a ritual surrounding it; it is usually drunk among friends, each of
them passing the *maté* on ceremoniously to the next.

yourselves, lads, this isn't the Scandinavian bourgeoisie, which agrees to sacrifice its profits in order to survive. The rich here will call in the military, even if the military then swallows them whole. Constitutionalists? Legalists? Will they feel shame or embarrassment at wearing a uniform or hiding their bald heads under helmets? Don't give me that, my dear compatriots. All that is in the past imperfect. They're going to strike and wipe us out as if we were Guatemalans. That's all there is to it. Which means we have to play the game against them on another pitch, away from the arena of mere political debate. We have to take them on and score goals against them, even if it's from outside the arena. That metaphor particularly pleased Santiago, who from then on started to show more interest. And Manolo went on and on, insisting they were all the same (*tango habemus*: 'A fly is the same as a cypress tree'),* because what he wanted more than anything was change, not just chit-chat about change, but change that was really real, to quote his words. And he wasn't that bothered about the means – 'If Jesus doesn't help, then the Devil will' – what was essential were the ends. That sounds familiar, Silvio commented with oblique irony. And you think we can kick them out? asked Santiago, who was the one drinking the *maté* now, but relatively quietly. No, Manolo replied without hesitation, as euphoric as if he were selling the future. No, we won't be able to, they're going to crush us, put us in jail, smash us to a pulp, annihilate us. So what, then? asked Silvio, his irony quickly turning to bewilderment. He, Rolando, had merely raised his eyebrows in healthy scepticism. So, then nothing, the speaker concluded exultantly.

* This is a quotation from a tango song called 'Cambalache' ('Pawnshop'), which was written in 1934 by Enrique Santos Discépolo. It's a bitter reflection that nothing has real value any more, that everything is the same and can be pawned or swapped for anything else.

Nothing in the short term, but the victory, their victory, will be a Pyrrhic one. They'll win, but won't know what to do with the trophy. They'll win on paper, but they'll lose the people. (A ripple of applause from the female seats.) So in the end they'll lose. Then, glancing provocatively at Silvio: Do you still reckon I'm nuts? Maybe we all are, said the other guy, conceding a little. So Manolo got up and gave him a hug befitting a cephalopod mollusc with eight tentacles, in other words an octopus, according to *Larousse*. Meanwhile, María del Carmen and Tita, who had recovered from the shock, were laughing with tears in their eyes, two rainbows. But Santiago was unusually serious and went on to argue that, expressed in those terms, the struggle was, simply, a moral one. What do I care about being an ethical victor if country clubs, big landowners and the banking clique and all the rest still exist? If I got into a fight like that I'd want to be a real winner. That's great, *che*, said Manolo. We'd all like to be real winners, don't imagine you're reinventing the wheel, it's a not matter of *wanting*, but of *being able* to do something about it. That made Silvio see red again, as he realized that from now on Manolo's aim was much broader: it had nothing to do with wanting or being able to do anything, the point was just to fuck everything up. Giggles from the female bench, and the gnocchi were ready – That's very quick, let's eat or they'll go soggy, my belly's full of *maté*, the thing is, you get into a heated argument and don't realize you've drunk two whole thermoses, what a bind. The gnocchi are waiting, gentlemen, this red wine is heavenly, it's sensational, so do you reckon that, come the revolution, there'll still be gnocchi?

Don Rafael
(God willing)

To close my eyes. How I'd love to close my eyes, start over and open them again with all the belated lucidity the years bring with them, but also with the youthful vitality I no longer have. 'You don't know what you've got till it's gone': God gives bread to the toothless. But before that, long before that, he gave hunger to those who did have teeth. What a great snare God is. In the end, sayings about the divine are like a kind of political primer: 'A godawful row': *Vehemence and fury.* 'God proposes and man disposes': *Conspiracy and harassment.* 'Render unto God what is God's and to Caesar what is Caesar's': *Carving up and sharing out.* 'With God on our side': *Dominance and empire.* 'Godforsaken': *Indifference and scorn.* 'Praise God and pass the ammunition': *Vigilantes, paramilitaries, death squads, etc.* 'It's in God's hands': *Absolute power.* 'God helps those who help themselves': *Neo-colonialism.* 'God separated the sheep from the goats': *Subliminal torture.* 'God be with you': *Bad company.*

To close my eyes. Not to return to the nightmares I have these days, but to get to the bottom of things. To where the images lie, the meaningful ones, the ones that are all mine. Each one like a revelation I neither understood nor heeded at the time. And there's no going back. You can piece together all you've learned, but there's not much use in that.

To close my eyes and, when I open them again, to find her there. Which one? One is a face. Another, a belly. Yet another, a glance. How many more? In love, there are no ridiculous, absurd or obscene postures. Without love everything is ridiculous and kitsch and obscene. Such is the case with rules, with traditions.

All of a sudden, the past becomes lavish, though I don't know why. The body I once had, the air I breathed, the sun that shone on me, the students I listened to, the pubis I won over, a twilight, an underarm, a nodding pine tree.

The past becomes resplendent and yet it's an optical illusion. Because the poor, dismal present wins a single, decisive battle: it exists. I am where I am. What is this exile, if not another beginning? And every beginning is youthful. So I, an old beginner, am growing young again. Having reached the stage of widower, veteran teacher, custodian of words, I'm condemned to grow young again. The last hurrah, the coda: I'm being fattened for the kill, as idiots say. But I'm still scrawny, *damn it*. In my country I used to complain, '*For heaven's sake*,' but I was scrawny there, too. From heaven to damnation, America is one giant homeland. And a son in prison. Imprisoned and wretchedly so, because he feels dynamic and optimistic and doesn't really have much to justify such an odd state of mind. And my own feelings are all over the place, damn it. I am where I am and he is where he is. My poor, wretched son. If only I could change places with him. But they won't have me. I'm not sufficiently hateful. I didn't want to overthrow them, disarm them, defeat them. He did, and he failed. If I could go in there and he could come out, maybe I wouldn't have such a bad time. I reckon that at sixty-seven they wouldn't torture me. Well, you never know. And there, too, I'd close my eyes and be free of the bars. And maybe I could get to the bottom of things. But no. I am where I am, and he is where he is. To close my eyes and see my son, but then to open them and see her. Which one?

Probably the one on the boat. Or the one by the tree. Or with the bird. God proposes and woman disposes. If I were God, I'd give strict orders for the one by the tree to appear. But since I'm not, it's Lydia who appears.

Battered and Bruised
(A terrible fear)

Graciela finished the second quarterly report. She took a deep breath before taking the original and seven copies out of the electric typewriter. There was no one else left in the office. She had worked three extra hours. Not for the money, but because her boss was in a tight spot and was a good sort and the next day was the deadline for the second quarter report.

She added the last sheet to the other thirty-three. First thing in the morning she would distribute the original and copies in eight folders. She was too tired now. She left everything in the second drawer, put the plastic cover on the typewriter and looked at her hands, blackened by the carbon paper.

She went into the washroom for a moment. She washed her hands methodically, combed her hair, touched up her lipstick. She studied herself in the mirror without smiling, but arching her eyebrows slightly, as if asking herself a question, or wondering about something, or simply confirming how tired she was. She pressed together her newly painted lips and sighed mildly. Then she returned to her desk, fished her bag out of the top drawer, took her coat from a hanger and put it on. She opened the door and went out into the corridor, but before she switched off the light and shut the door again she glanced round the room. Everything as it should be.

When the lift door opened she got a surprise. She wasn't

expecting to see anyone, but there was Celia, as taken aback as she was.

'I haven't seen you for ages. What are you doing in the office at this time of night?'

'I had to type up the report for the second quarter. And it was incredibly long.'

'You do your boss too many favours. One of these days you'll end up going to bed with him.'

'No, sweetheart, there's no danger of that. He's not my type. But he's a good sort. Besides, he didn't even ask me to do the work. And anyway, he wasn't even in the office.'

'Darling, you needn't justify yourself so much. It was a joke.'

They emerged into the street. It was foggy, to the car drivers' exasperation.

'Would you like some tea?'

'Not exactly tea. But maybe a drink. It'd do me good after my thirty-four pages and seven copies.'

'That's what I like to hear. Long live escape!'

They sat next to a window. From a nearby table a young, sprucely dressed man cast a calculating eye over them.

'Well,' Celia said in a low voice, 'it seems we're still worth looking at.'

'Does that make you feel good or depress you?'

'I'm not sure. It depends a lot on my state of mind. And also on what the person giving me the once-over is like.'

'And this one in particular, does he make you feel good?'

'No.'

'Thank heavens.'

The waiter gently deposited their two drinks on the table.

'Here's to our health.'

'To our health and freedom.'

'Sure, that covers it all.'

'Actually, I think that was one of Artigas's* slogans.'

'Really? How'd you know?'

'If you'd lived all the years I've lived with Santiago, you'd be an expert in Artigas as well. He was always one of his obsessions.'

Celia took a sip of her drink.

'What's the latest from him?'

'The same as ever. He writes regularly, except when he's being punished for something. He's in good spirits.'

'Is there any hope they might let him out?'

'There's good grounds to. But not much hope.'

At this time of day, the life on the street outside was hypnotic. The two women sat for a while in silence, staring out at the cars, the packed buses, the ladies walking dogs, beggars with their handwritten signs, ragged children, smart young men, the police. Celia was the first to tear herself away from the busy spectacle.

'What about you? How do you feel? How are you coping with such a long separation?' Celia paused. 'You don't have to answer if you don't want to.'

'The thing is, I'd like to give you an answer. The problem is, I don't have one.'

'You don't know how you feel?'

'I feel unbalanced, disoriented, insecure.'

'That's only logical, isn't it?'

'Possibly. But it doesn't seem so logical when I want to answer your second question. About how I'm coping with the separation.'

'Why, what's happening?'

---

* One of the leaders of the fight for the independence of Uruguay in the early nineteenth century.

'What's happening is, quite simply, that I *am* coping. Far too well. And that's not normal.'

'I don't understand you, Graciela.'

'You know what a good couple Santiago and I made. And you know how in tune we were when it came to politics. We were both into the same thing. Even with him in prison and me here. When they took him, I thought I'd find it unbearable. We weren't just united physically: it was spiritual. You can't imagine how much I needed him at first.'

'But not any longer?'

'It's not that simple. I still love him. How couldn't I, after ten years of a wonderful relationship? And I find it horrible that he's in jail. I'm also perfectly aware of the impact that his absence is having on Beatriz as she grows up.'

'Yes, all that's on one side of the scales. And on the other?'

'The problem is that our forced separation has made him more tender. Whereas it's made me tougher. To cut a long story short (and this is something I haven't confessed to anyone: I find it hard even to confess to myself), I need him less and less.'

'Graciela.'

'I know what you're going to say: that it's unfair. I know that perfectly well. I'm not so stupid I don't realize that.'

'Graciela.'

'But I can't deceive myself. I still feel a great affection for him, but as a fellow revolutionary, not as his wife. He misses my body – he's always hinting at it in his letters – but I don't feel any need for his. And that makes me feel – how can I put it? – it makes me feel guilty. Because in fact I haven't the faintest idea what is happening to me.'

'There could be an explanation.'

'Of course, you think there's someone else. But there isn't.'

'Are you sure?'

'There isn't yet.'

'Why did you add that *yet*?'

'Because there could be at any moment. That fact that I don't feel a need for Santiago's body doesn't mean mine is lifeless. I haven't made love to anyone in more than four years, Celia. Doesn't that seem a bit much to you?'

'I really have no idea.'

'Of course, you have Pedro with you. And things are going well. Fortunately. But how can you know what would have happened to you if you had spent four years without seeing or touching him, or being seen and touched by him?'

'I don't know, and I don't want to know.'

'I think it's good, you refusing to get pointlessly involved in someone else's drama. But I'm quite sure of what's happening to me. I can't help but know. And I can assure you it's not easy, or comfortable or pleasant.'

'And haven't you thought of telling him little by little, letter by letter?'

'Of course, I've thought of it. And it makes me very afraid.'

'Afraid? Of what?'

'Of destroying him. Of destroying myself. I don't know.'

Intramural
(The bonus)

Having news from you is like opening a window. What you tell me about yourself, Beatriz, the old man, your work, the city. I know your schedules, and I can visualize all your routines, so at any moment I can organize my imaginary world: now Graciela is typing, or the old man is finishing his class right now, or Beatriz is gulping down her breakfast because she's late for school. When you've no choice but to stay in one place, you build up incredible mental agility. You can stretch out in the present as much as you like, or dizzily pitch yourself into the future, or you can slide into reverse: that's dangerous, though, because it's where your memories are, all of them: the good, the insignificant and the downright horrible. That's where love is, in other words, where you are, darling, and where the great loyalties and great betrayals lie. That's where you find what you could have done, but didn't do, as well as what you could have not done, but did. The crossroads where you chose the wrong path. And that's where the film begins; I mean, the story of how things would have been if you had turned and changed direction, taken another path, the one you rejected at the time. In general, after several reels you stop the projection and conclude that maybe the path you chose wasn't such a mistake after all and that maybe, faced with the same crossroads, you'd choose the same one again. With a few differences, of course. With less naivety, for sure. And more caution, just in case. And yet keeping on in that same original direction.

These long periods of nothingness do tend to be demoralizing, but taken from another angle they can also be quite positive. In those last few moments before the arrests, everything happened in such a rush and there was so much tension, we were engulfed by so many inescapable crises, by so many decisions to be made, that none of us had the time or the inclination to just stop and think, to consider and reconsider the steps we were taking, to achieve any mental clarity. Now there's time, too much time, too many sleepless nights, nights with the same nightmares, the same shadows. And it's only natural (and very easy) to ask yourself: What good does time do me now? What's the point of all this overdue contemplation? It's anachronistic, it's come too late, pointless. And yet it does have its uses. The only value this empty time has is the possibility of maturing, learning your own limits, your weaknesses and strengths, getting a bit closer to the truth about yourself – not to having any illusions about goals you're never going to achieve – but instead readying your mind, sorting out your approach to life and building up your patience so that you will be able to achieve what might, one day, be within your grasp. And, in these extraordinary circumstances, you can delve so deep in your inquiry that – I'll risk confessing something to you – although I can't draw up a five-year plan of my nightmares, I can dream with my eyes open, chapter by chapter. I can pick apart and examine what I once wanted and what I want now, what I have done and what I will do. Because one day I'll be able to do things again, won't I? One day I'll leave behind this strange exile and become part of the world again, no? And I'll be a different person, possibly even someone better, although I'll never become an enemy of the person I once was, or who I am now; it will be a sort of bonus. Yes, receiving news from you is like opening a window, but then I feel an almost irrepressible urge to open more windows, and what's worse (sheer madness), to open a door. And yet I'm condemned always to see the back of this door: hostile, harsh, impregnable, all too solid – although it's never as solid as a good argument, a solid reason. Getting news from you is like opening a window. But not yet like opening a door. Maybe I've used that word *door* too often, but you have to understand, it's almost an obsession; more so, even though you may not believe it, than the word *bar*. The bars are there, they're a real, unavoidable presence in all their dreary magnitude. But bars can't be anything other than what they so obviously are. You can't have open bars and closed bars. But a door can be so many things. When it's closed (as it always is), it signifies enclosure, prohibition, silence, rage. If it were open (not opened for an exercise period or for work or punishment – those are simply other ways of being shut in – but open to the world) that would mean recovering reality, loved ones, streets, tastes, smells, sounds, images and the feeling of being free. It would, for example, be to get you back, your arms, your mouth, your hair and – Bah! why try to open a bolt that won't budge, a jammed lock? The fact is that the word *door* is one you hear most often here, even more than those other words that are behind the door. That's because we know that to reach them, to reach the words *child, wife, friend, street, bed, café, library, square, football stadium, port, telephone*, first of all, you have to get beyond the word *door*. And this door, which always has its back turned on us but which is always there, staring at us coldly, cruelly and so very solid, refusing to make any promises or offer any hope, always slamming in our faces. And yet we don't allow ourselves to be defeated so easily; we organize our campaign for release. We write letters, bearing in mind both our recipient and the censor, or we plan letters in which usually we carry on censoring ourselves, but are a little more daring, or we chew over monologues like this one, which won't ever reach a scrap of paper with its limitations. But one of the most noteworthy, most positive parts of our campaign is precisely that we make ourselves promises, set ourselves goals (not unbelievable, triumphalist ones, but limited, achievable ones), just imagining we're opening the door right in front of us. Sometimes, though not always, we'll have a pack of cards or chess. Ah, but we also have the right to play at the future, and naturally in that game of chance we always keep a card up our sleeve, or keep a secret surprise, an incredibly original checkmate that we won't waste on daily games, but rather put aside for a great occasion, for example, when we face Capablanca or Alekhine, better not mention Karpov, because, after all, he's still alive and, besides, his name could yet be scrubbed out. We also talk about music and musicians, so long as the music doesn't transport me and whatever cellmate I have somewhere else. But, on my own or with somebody to talk to, I can, for example, recall many of my highlights as a listener, a spectator. And so I tell him (or, at my most hermitic moments, tell myself) the story of how I saw and heard Maurice Chevalier at the Teatro Solís: even though by that time he was a grizzled veteran, he was still good-humoured and charming enough to make us all believe he was improvising each and every one of his antediluvian jokes. I also saw and heard Louis Armstrong in the Plaza Hotel and still I can hear that gruff growl, its irresistible humanity. I also saw and heard Charles Trenet, in I don't know which Spanish centre on Calle Soriano, everyone perched on what looked like dining-chairs while we kids sat on the floor, and the Frenchie, rather mannered but a consummate artist, was singing a song that years later I found out was called 'La Mer' or 'Bonsoir, jolie madame'. And I saw and heard Marian Anderson, I can't remember whether in the Sodre or the Solís, but I clearly see

the figure of that enormous, gentle black woman, her incanta-
tory voice embodying the tragic destiny of her race; and many
years later I saw and heard Robbe-Grillet, announcing emphat-
ically that in Camus's *L'Etranger* the use of the past imperfect
tense was more important than the plot; and I saw and heard
Mercedes Sosa singing totally alone, in an almost clandestine
way, in the Zitlovsky Jewish Cultural Institute on Calle
Durazno; and saw and heard Roa Bastos, modest to a fault, telling a shamefully small audience that Paraguay has had to live
as if it's always Year Zero; and I saw and heard Don Ezequiel
Martínez Estrada, a few months before his death, giving a lec-
ture on a topic I don't recall because I was concentrating so
hard on his gaunt, sallow, parchment-dry face, where the only
sign of life was the sharp, darting gaze of his tiny eyes; and I
saw and heard Neftalí Ricardo Reyes,* jokey, ironic, subtly
vain and every inch the poet, reciting his memories of Isla
Negra like a psalm; and when I was in the midst of an audience
I saw the one from the other island† on the Esplanada, stirred
by the length, drive and style of the unexpected concert, which
for so many others was disconcerting. Memories of a child,
adolescent and grown man, but beyond any doubt, memories
of mine. In other words, when I raise the curtain, I am, as you
may have appreciated, oh so interesting, I applaud myself and
demand, Encore, Encore, Encore.

* The real name of the Chilean poet Pablo Neruda.
† The 'one from the other island' is Fidel Castro, who visited Uruguay in 1959.

Exiles
(Man in a doorway)

I had met President Siles Zuazo in Montevideo some twenty years earlier, when he came to Uruguay as an exile following the success of one of the many military coups that have continually scarred the history of Bolivia. Back then, I had only published a few books, and was working in the accounts department of a big real estate company.

One afternoon the phone rang at my desk and a deep voice said, 'Siles Zuazo here.' At first I thought it was a joke and yet, perhaps aware of the remote possibility it was true, I didn't answer in kind. I was still recovering from the shock when he managed to convince me who he was. In fact, he was inviting me to go and see him at the Hotel Nogaró. I thought he probably wanted to talk about Bolivia and the officers who had seized power there, but I couldn't work out why he had chosen me in particular. I was mistaken.

A few years earlier I had published an essay on 'Marcel Proust and the Sense of Guilt'. And Siles Zuazo wanted to chat with me about Proust and other literary topics. I discovered that this statesman of a land cut off from the sea, this character, tales of whose great civic valour had been related to me by several friends, was an exceptionally cultured man, a devoted reader of contemporary literature.

Obviously, we talked of Proust while we drank tea with toast. We were missing only the madeleines. Politics was mentioned a handful of times, only because of questions that I had asked. Really, he wanted to talk about literature, and his remarks were unquestionably perceptive and wise.

Following this first meeting, we had tea on several occasions in the Nogaró, and I have lasting warm memories of our tranquil conversations. Soon afterwards, he left Montevideo to rejoin the struggles and political vicissitudes of his irreplaceable Bolivia.

I didn't see him for many years, although I always followed news of his tireless political activity: lawful whenever possible, clandestine when it wasn't. One night of pouring rain in Buenos Aires, back in 1974, I was walking, I think, down Calle Paraguay looking for shelter when, all of a sudden, as I rushed past a doorway, I thought I recognized a man standing there, taking cover from the storm.

I looked back. It was Dr Siles. He had recognized me as well. 'So. Now it's your turn living in exile.' 'Yes. When we used to talk in Montevideo that seemed quite impossible, didn't it?' 'Yes, so it seemed.' In the half-darkness I couldn't quite make out his smile, but I could imagine it. 'And, in your unexpected exile, what stage is this?' 'The third,' I replied, a little ashamed. 'Don't take it too badly. I'm on my fourteenth.'

That night we didn't talk of Proust.

Beatriz
(This country)

This country isn't mine, but I like it a lot. I don't know if I like it more or less than my own country. I came here when I was very little and can't remember what that was like any more. One of the differences is that in my country there are horses and here they are hosses. But they all neigh. Cows moo and frogs croak.

This country is bigger than mine, mainly because mine is so tiny. In this country live my Grandpa Rafael and my mum Graciela. And millions more. It's very nice to know one lives in a country with many millions. When Graciela takes me to the centre, loads of people are in the streets. There are so many many many people that it seems to me I must know all the millions in this country.

On Sundays the streets are almost empty and I wonder where all the millions I saw on Friday can have got to. My Grandpa Rafael says that on Sundays people stay at home to rest. To rest means to sleep.

There's a lot of sleep in this country. Especially on Sundays, because there are many millions asleep. If each sleeping person snores nine times an hour (my mum snores fourteen times) that means each million inhabitants snore nine million times an hour. In other words, snores abound.

Sometimes when I sleep I start to dream. I almost always dream of this country, but some nights I dream of my own country. Graciela says that can't be right because I don't remember it. But when I dream I do remember, even if Graciela says I'm making it up. I'm not making it up.

I dream that my dad takes me by the hand and we visit Villa Dolores – that's the name of the zoo. And he buys me peanuts to feed to the monkeys, and those monkeys aren't the ones in the zoo here because I know these monkeys very well and also their wives and children. The monkeys in my dreams are those in Villa Dolores. My dad says, Beatriz, can you see those bars, that's how I'm living now. Then I wake up crying in this country and Graciela has to come and tell me, Sweetheart, it's only a dream.

I say that it's a shame that among the millions of people in this country, for example, my father isn't one of them.

Battered and Bruised
(Daydreaming)

'See, that's why I don't want you to go to school on your own.'

'What did I do?'

'Don't act all innocent.'

'But what did I do?'

'You were going to cross on a red light.'

'There weren't any cars coming.'

'Yes, there were, Beatriz.'

'Only in the distance.'

'Now we can cross.'

They walked past the supermarket, then the dry-cleaner's.

'Graciela.'

'What is it?'

'I promise I'll always cross with the green light.'

'You already promised me that last week.'

'But now I really mean it. Do you forgive me?'

'It's not about forgiving or not forgiving. Don't you realize that if you cross when the light's red you could be knocked down by a car?'

'Yes, you're right.'

'What will I do, Beatriz, if anything happens to you? Don't you ever think of that?'

'Nothing's going to happen to me, Mum. Please don't cry. I'll always cross with the green light. Graciela. Mum. Don't cry.'

'I'm not crying any more, silly. Come on, in you go.'

'It's still early. Class begins in twenty minutes. And the sunshine is lovely. I want to spend a bit longer with you.'

'Now you're buttering me up.' As she says this, Graciela relaxes a little and smiles.

'Have you forgiven me?'

'Yes.'

'Are you going to your office now?'

'No.'

'Are you on holiday?'

'I worked a lot last week so they've given me this Monday off.'

'What are you going to do? Are you going to the movies?'

'I don't think so. I reckon I'll go home.'

'Will you come to fetch me after school? Or can I come back on my own?'

'I'd like to be able to trust you.'

'You can, Mum. Nothing's going to happen to me. Really.'

Beatriz doesn't wait for Graciela's reply. Brushing her cheek with a kiss, she runs into school. Graciela stands there for a while, watching her disappear. Then she purses her lips and leaves.

She walks slowly, swinging her handbag. She stops occasionally, as though disoriented. When she reaches the main avenue, she gazes at the row of tall buildings. Suddenly the people crossing the road brush past her, jostle her, mutter. Finally, she makes up her mind and crosses, too. Before she reaches the opposite pavement, the light has turned red and a truck has had to swerve to avoid her.

Now she turns down an almost deserted street, where there are several large rubbish bins, overflowing, stinking. She approaches one and peers in. She makes as if to put her hand in, but then pulls back.

She walks two, three, five, ten blocks. On the corner before the next avenue, there's a woman begging. Two very young children are dozing beside her. Graciela approaches her and the woman starts with her refrain once again.

'Why are you begging, eh?'

The woman looks at her in astonishment. She is used to people giving, refusing or walking straight past. Never conversation.

'What?'

'I'm asking why you beg.'

'So that I can eat, señora. For the love of God.'

'Can't you work?'

'No, señora. For the love of God.'

'You can't or you won't?'

'No, señora.'

'No, what?'

'There's no work. For the love of God.'

'Leave the love of God out of it. Don't you realize that God doesn't have love for you?'

'Don't say that, señora. Don't say that.'

'Here.'

'Thank you, señora. For the love of God.'

She walks on more determinedly. Leaving the beggar woman behind her, bewildered. One of her children starts to cry. Graciela turns her head to look back at them, but doesn't stop.

When she is two blocks from home, she dimly makes out Rolando, in the distance, leaning against her front door. She walks another block towards him and waves. He doesn't seem to spot her. She repeats the gesture and then he responds, waves and starts coming towards her.

'How did you know I was coming home?'

'Simple. I called your office and they told me you weren't coming in today.'

'I almost went to the movies.'

'Yes, I thought you might. But it's so sunny I didn't think you'd want to shut yourself up in a cinema. So I came down here, and as you see, I was right.'

He kisses her on both cheeks. She rummages in her bag, finds her key and opens the door.

'Come in, sit down. Something to drink?'

'No, nothing.'

Graciela draws back the shutters and takes off her coat. Rolando looks at her, curious.

'Have you been crying?'

'Is it that obvious?'

'You have a look that's technically known as "after the storm".'

'Bah, it was only a light shower.'

'What's wrong?'

'Not much. An unjustified moment of despair with a beggar woman and, before that, a justified moment of anger at Beatriz.'

'Beatriz? She's so sweet.'

'She's a very good girl. But she always outmanoeuvres me.'

'So what happened?'

'It was my own fault. She's so careless when she crosses the street, it scares me.'

'Is that all?'

Rolando offers her a cigarette, but she refuses. He takes one and lights it. Blowing out the first lungful, he peers at her through the smoke.

'Graciela, when are you going to make your mind up?'

'About what?'

'About whether you'll confess to yourself. The thing, whatever it is, that you don't want to admit.'

'Don't start, Rolando. I can't stand that paternalistic tone of yours.'

'I've known you a long time, Graciela. Longer than Santiago.'

'That's true.'

'And since I know you, I can tell when you're feeling bad.'

'I am.'

'And you'll go on feeling that way until you admit it to yourself.'

'Possibly. But it's difficult. It's hard.'

'I know.'

'It's about Santiago.'

'Ah.'

'And above all, about me. Bah, it's not that complicated. But it's hard. I don't know what's happening to me, Rolando. That's what's so difficult to admit. The fact is, I don't need Santiago any more.'

'And how long have you felt like this?'

'Don't ask for precise dates. How do I know? It's absurd.'

'Don't put a label on it yet.'

'It is absurd, Rolando. Santiago didn't do anything. Except get taken prisoner. What d'you make of that? Can you think of anything more cruel, anything worse, you can do to a person? That's what he did to me. He got taken prisoner. He abandoned me.'

'He didn't abandon you, Graciela. He was taken away.'

'I know. That's why I say it's absurd. I know he got taken away and yet I feel as though he abandoned me.'

'And you blame him for that?'

'No, how am I going to blame him? He behaved well, impeccably: he withstood torture, he was brave, he didn't betray anyone. He's to be looked up to.'

'And yet?'

'And yet I've been distancing myself. And the distance has given me the chance to reconsider our whole relationship.'

'Which was a good one.'

'A really good one.'

'Well, then?'

'It isn't any more. He goes on writing me affectionate, warm and tender letters, but I read them as if they were addressed to someone else. Can you tell me what's happened? Can it be that prison has changed Santiago into another person? Can it be I've been transformed, by exile, into a different woman?'

'It's all possible. But it could all be enriching for both of you. Better.'

'I haven't grown better and I don't feel enriched. I feel poorer, withered. And I don't want to go on growing poorer or withering any further.'

'Graciela. Do you still share Santiago's political convictions?'

'Of course. They're mine too, aren't they? Except that he was caught. Whereas I am here.'

'Do you resent the commitments he made?'

'Are you crazy? He did what he had to. So did I. You're barking up the wrong tree. In that sense we were and still are united. Where I'm not united with him is in the relationship between the two of us. Not in social matters – in conjugal ones, if you follow me. I'm clear about that, at least. What I'm not clear about is the reason why. And that worries me. If Santiago had done something dreadful to me, or if I'd seen him do something dreadful to another person . . . But no, he's beyond reproach. Loyal, a good friend, a good companion, a good husband. And I was very much in love with him.'

'What about him?'

'The same. Apparently, he still feels the same. I'm the one who's crazy.'

'Graciela. You're still young. You're pretty, intelligent, sometimes even tender. Perhaps what you're missing is a kind of response, a sense that your feelings are reciprocated.'

'My. It's so difficult.'

'That's something Santiago can't give you in his letters, still less if they're censored.'

'Perhaps.'

'Can I ask you a really indiscreet question?'

'You can. But I might not answer.'

'All right.'

'What is it, then?'

'Do you dream of other men?'

'Do you mean erotic dreams?'

'Yes.'

'Sleeping, or daydreaming?'

'Both.'

'When I'm asleep, I don't dream about any man.'

'And when you're awake?'

'When I'm awake, I do daydream. You're going to laugh. I dream of you.'

Don Rafael
(Benign and cruel madmen)

Santiago wrote, and he's fine. I've learned to read between the lines – his lines – so I know he's still in his right mind. That's been my fear. Not that he'll talk, or weaken. No. I think I know my son. My fear has been that he'll slip from sanity to who knows what. The prison governor (I don't know if it was the current one, or the one before him) once put it like this: 'We didn't dare finish them all off when we had the chance, and, at some point, we'll have to set them free. We have to use the time we've got left to drive them all insane.' At least he was frank about it, wasn't he? Frank and deplorable. But something in that shameless remark hit home: it's in them, those blood-hounds, there's something crazy in them. They are the ones who are spending the time left going insane. But they're not benign madmen; they're twisted, grotesque. Madmen by voca-tion and free choice, which is the cruellest kind of madness. They were given scholarships to Fort Gulick and they gradu-ated as madmen. Even though the prison governor said it more than five years ago, I still cling to the only words that offer any hope in his chilling summary. 'We'll have to set them free.' So they 'didn't dare finish off' Santiago when they 'had the chance'. But will he be among those they set free before he is driven mad? I hope so. Santiago has managed to generate, or maybe to discover within himself, a strange vitality. His descent into hell has not burned him. Singed, perhaps. I think that in there, even more than clinging to hope, what's important is to hang on to your sanity. And he is still sane. Touch wood. And, just in case, wood without legs: this olive-wood spoon, for example, which is, moreover, a gift from Lydia. Santiago is still sane because he has deliberately clung on to his sanity. And he is dosing his hatreds prudently and wisely: that's all-important. Hatred only enlivens and stimulates you if you're able to control it; if you can't, it will destroy and unhinge you. I know it's hard to keep your common sense about you when you've suffered relentless humiliation and silence, when you've been nauseated by death, unending terror and dread, on behalf of others: martyrdom on an instalment plan. After enduring all that, staying sane can be a kind of delirium. That's the only way to explain such an obstinate commitment to mental balance. And sticking to your principles, of course. But there were people with many solid and proclaimed principles who still weakened and ended up feeling like shit. People I'm not judging: let that be clear to everyone and to myself, because nobody knows who they really are, how flammable or fire-resistant they are, until they've been through the fire. I'll be frank: of course, principles are a fundamental part of it, but they're only one part. The rest is self-respect, loyalty to others and above all a lot of pig-headedness, and also, it occurs to me now, a progressive demystifying of death. Because that's the most powerful, piercing argument they wield: the genuine likelihood, the looming presence, of death – not just any death, one's own death. And it's only by taking death down a notch, deflating its legendary reputation, that man can win the struggle. He must convince himself that to die is not, after all, that terrible, provided he dies a good death, dies at peace with himself. And yet it also occurs to me (I who have never had to run that risk) that it can't be easy, because in a situation like that you are agonizingly alone, not even accompanied by the grimy presence of the ceiling or walls, or the despicable faces of those who are destroying you. You are alone with the hood over your head, or rather, with the inside of a sack; alone with your pounding heart, your retching, your suffocation, your never-ending anguish. Obviously, once this is over, when it's all done with and you become conscious of having survived it all, you must be left with a crumb of dignity, but also a permanent deposit of rancour. Which will never go away, even if the future brings you security, trust, love and a safe path forward. A deposit of rancour that can rot and spread and even contaminate that trust and love, that onward path, all of which could intertwine with more than one individual future. In other words, those ruthless jailers, those experts in cruelty, those loathsome cannibals, those hierophants of the Sacred Order of the Trap, are guilty not only in the present; their guilt will carry far into the future. Not only are they responsible for every single iniquity, or for the sum of those iniquities; they are responsible, also, for having undermined the time honoured foundations of a solid society. When they torture a person, kill him or not, they are also tormenting (even though they don't lock them up, even if they just leave them defenceless and bewildered in their ravaged homes) that person's wife, his parents, his children, damaging all of their relationships. When they crush a revolutionary (as in the case of Santiago) and force his family into exile, they tear time to shreds; distorting the history of that branch of the tree, that small clan. To regroup in exile is not, as is so often said, to wipe the slate clean, to start the count again from zero. You start from minus four, or minus twenty, or minus a hundred. The ruthless ones, the ones who really earned their stripes in militant cruelty, who started out as puritans and ended up utterly corrupt, have opened a long parenthesis in our society, a parenthesis that will surely be closed some day, although by then nobody will be able to pick up the thread of the original sentence. A new one will have to be woven, constructed with words that will no longer be the same (because beautiful words were among the properties of those whom they tortured, executed or added to the lists of the disappeared) in which subjects and prepositions and transitive verbs and direct objects will no longer be the same. The syntax will have changed in this society, born as it will be by Caesarean section. At its birth, it will seem weak, anaemic, hesitant, far too cautious, but over time it will come together, invent new rules and new exceptions, brand-new words will rise from the ashes of those prematurely burned, copulative conjunctions better able to act as bridges between those who stayed and those who left and will then return. But nothing will be able to stay as it was before 1973. For better or for worse; I'm not sure. And I'm even less sure that I'll be able to grow accustomed (if I do return some day) to that transformed country, the one that's even now being born in the backroom of the forbidden. Yes, it's likely that my dis-exile will be as hard as exile. The new society will not be built by veterans like me, or even by mature youngsters like Rolando or Graciela. We're survivors, of course, but we're also battered and bruised. Them, and us. So will it be built by those who today are children, like my granddaughter? I don't know, I really don't know. Maybe the new celebrants, the future makers of that strange, suspended homeland will be those who are children today but who live, still, in the home country. Not the young boys and girls whose retinas absorb images of the snows of Oslo or sunsets over the Mediterranean or the pyramids of Teotihuacán or scooters on the Via Appia or the dark skies of the Swedish winter. Nor the young boys and girls who have memories of children begging in the Alameda, or the Latin Quarter drug addicts, or the consumer frenzy of Caracas or Tejero's attempted coup in Madrid or the neo-Nazi disruptions of the German miracle. At most, they may be able to help, to communicate some of what they've learned, delve into what has been forgotten, try to adapt and work hard. But those who will forge the new, strange country of the foreseeable future, that homeland that is yet an enigma, will be today's adolescents, those who were there, and who are there still, those who saw it as children, not amnesiacs, who saw so much of the bitter fighting and who, like other adolescents, those of '69 and '70, were riddled with bullets, declared to be enemies, who saw how their fathers, uncles and sometimes their mothers and even their grandparents were taken away, only to be seen again much, much later on, from behind bars, or from afar or, even, at close quarters, but kept remote by the impossible task of communicating, by emotional distance. And they saw people weeping, and themselves wept beside coffins they were forbidden to peer into, and witnessed the deafening silence on street corners that ensued, and the scissors that cut off their hair and their conversation, and yes, of course, took to rock music and jukeboxes and slot machines to forget the unforgettable. I've no idea how or when, but those kids of today will become the vanguard of a realistic uprising. What about us veterans? We the hearses, as the Spaniards say. Well, those of us who are still lucid by then, may we hearses still roll along, we'll help them remember what they saw. And what they didn't see.

Exiles
(Immobile solitude)

Journalist H., an expert in international affairs and correspondent for a Bulgarian newspaper in Montevideo, ended up in Sofia. After one of the Uruguayan regime's many attacks, he had been forced to seek exile in Argentina, where he lived for seven months. But following the assassination of Zelmar Michelini and Gutiérrez Ruiz, Argentina also became uninhabitable for Uruguayan exiles. Under the protection of the United Nations, he left for Cuba and, from there, went on to Bulgaria.

He lived alone, far from his wife and children, but doubtless he made friends among the Bulgarians, a warm and welcoming people, fond of noble, sentimental drinking. He must also have enjoyed those incredible avenues lined with rose-filled flowerbeds that can be found all over that beautiful country, which is, of course, Dimitrov's, but which also is that of my friend Vasil Popov, who more than ten years ago wrote a very tender story about two Tupamaros he once met in the lift of a Havana hotel.

Yes, he must surely have got used to yoghurt (from its home country), Orthodox priests and Turkish coffee, which I find undrinkable. But even so he must have doubtless felt the unpleasant humiliation of being utterly alone, looking at himself each day in the mirror with fresh astonishment and jaded resignation.

When in mid-1977 I arrived in Sofia to attend the Congress of Writers for Peace, H., ever the journalist, had made the news himself, just a few days earlier. As he did every evening, he had gone back to his apartment. He probably lay down, and nothing more was heard of him until a few days later, when his work colleagues, alarmed by his unexplained absence, went to knock on his door. Hearing no reply, they called the police to open it.

H. was in his bed, still alive, but in a coma. He had been left hemiplegic by some kind of cerebral collapse. He had been in this state for at least three days. Intensive care could do nothing for him.

Strictly speaking, he did not die of hemiplegia, but of solitude. The doctors said that, had he been found in time, he would probably have survived. By the time his friends found him, he had already lost consciousness – but it's likely that for at least twenty-four hours he knew what was happening to him. It's heart-rending, trying to grasp what his thoughts must have been as he lay there immobile. Out of respect, I won't do so, even though perhaps I am particularly suited to the task.

A couple of years earlier, during my Buenos Aires exile, in my solitary apartment on Las Heras and Pueyrredón, I had undergone a very similar episode. For a whole day, an asthma attack left me semi-conscious. Apparently, several friends called me, but I was unaware of this, even though the phone was by my bed. They must have thought I wasn't there. In those dark months of López Rega's* Argentina, when every day ten or twenty dead bodies appeared on rubbish tips, it was common for many of us, during especially worrying nights, to sleep at friends' houses. I always had at least three of their keys on my keyring. In the evening, I vaguely recovered consciousness. I answered a call, just one, before blacking out again. That single act was enough to save me. H. didn't even have that opportunity. Solitude had left him immobile.

---

* José López Rega was the Minister of Social Welfare during the Peronist government of 1973 to 1975, and one of those responsible for the killings by the right-wing Alianza Anti-Comunista Argenta (the Argentine Anti-Communist Alliance).

The Other
(First choice and substitute)

Little Beatriz is lightning-quick. If only Santiago could see her: Rolando knows her absence must have been the toughest test for that famous swot. Years without Beatriz; who knows how many. It seems there's some hope now, but what then? Obviously, Santiago will have other grounds for homesickness, Graciela being one of them, of course, but the hardest to accept must be Beatriz, because when he was rounded up he was just beginning to enjoy her. Not a lot, clearly, because those were dreadful years, but even so he found time to see her every two or three days. He'd bring her into the big bed and clown around with the kid, who ever since she was a little tadpole had been razor-sharp. Santiago was a devoted father, not like him, Rolando Asuero, *habitué* at first of brothels and then of motel rooms. It was really the politics that put a stop to his Latin American way of life: why, in the final days, even motel rooms were used for underground meetings. What a waste. He always felt a bit embarrassed not to even take off his jacket since he was obliged to respect the female comrade who would inevitably be there (*tango habemus*: 'I've only myself to blame, what a fool') in that classically celebratory ambience, although occasionally the context did win out over the text, but anyway it always seemed to him it was an abuse of authority by the irresponsible Responsible Ones, because in general the female comrades were gorgeous and you had to be really careful not to get aroused, you had to concentrate so hard on thinking of blocks of ice and snowy peaks that you'd end up forgetting the very message you had been given and were supposed to pass on.

A sharp one, little Beatriz. Today while they were both waiting for Graciela he had spent a good few minutes chatting with her. Rolando is enchanted by the way the kid talks about her mother, how she has got her worked out to a T, how she knows what's non-negotiable and what her weak spots are. The curious thing is that she talks of all this without vanity or boasting, with an almost scientific rigour. A rigour that vanishes as soon as she starts talking about Santiago. She has made him into a god. Today she cross-examined Rolando, her Uncle Rolando (to her, all Graciela's male friends are uncles; the female ones, aunts) asking him about 'the Prison', what the cells would be like, if it's true Santiago can see the sky (he says he can, but she says perhaps that's only so that Graciela and I don't cry), and why exactly he was in jail if both Graciela and he, her Uncle Rolando, assured her he was such a good person and loved his country so much. At that point she had fallen silent, before asking, eyes half-shut, focusing on a concern that doubtless was not new: 'Uncle, which is *my* country? I know yours is Uruguay, but what about me, I left there when I was tiny, so tell me truthfully, which is *my* country?' And when she said 'my' she prodded herself in the chest with her forefinger, and he had been forced to clear his throat and even blow his nose to give himself time before he told her that there could be people, especially children, who had two countries, one the first choice and the other the substitute. But then the kid started insisting, So which one was her first choice?, and he said, Obviously, that's Uruguay, then she jabbed her finger in the wound – So why then don't I remember anything about my first-choice country, but on the other hand know lots about my substitute country? And thank heavens Graciela arrived at that moment and opened the door (they were waiting by the window, unable to get in) and went to wash her hands and run a comb through her hair, and told Beatriz to wash her hands too, and the kid: I already washed them at midday, so Graciela got mad and dragged her roughly to the washbasin, then came back in a state to where Rolando was sitting in the rocking-chair, staring at him as if it were only now that she had become aware of his presence and saying, Hello, in a weary, defenceless voice that bore only a distant resemblance to her normal one.

Intramural
(The seaside resort)

I don't know why today I had such vivid memories of the sum-
mers at Solís. The cabin there was lovely, so close to the beach.
Sometimes when I lose my patience or grow angry, I think of
the sand dunes and quieten down. In those short seasons of
calm, which so closely resembled happiness, who could have
imagined everything that was about to happen? I remember
when we climbed the sierra, and when we met Sonia and
Rubén, when we rented horses and you were firm in the saddle
when it trotted, but despite all your commands and efforts the
pony wouldn't break into a gallop, which meant you ended up
shattered. And yet I don't just remember those bucolic seaside
details; I also recall feeling a certain uneasiness that meant I
couldn't entirely enjoy those three weeks of frugal comfort.
Do you remember what we talked about, so often, as evening
drew in around the cabin and the hour of the *angelus* made
us melancholy, gloomy, even? Yes, our comfort was terribly
austere, our little getaway was extremely cheap and far from
ostentatious, and yet we couldn't help thinking of all those
who had nothing, no work or bread or anywhere to live,
still less a special hour given over to melancholy; their bitterness was full-time. And so we'd end up sitting in silence, with
no obvious solutions to hand, feeling vaguely guilty. Of course,
by the next morning when the fresh salty air and the first rays
of the sun filled the cabin at dawn, nature's encouragement

chased away our dark thoughts and we'd feel replete and optimistic again. You'd spend your time collecting shells, while I
went out on the bike, because even back then you maintained
I had a certain tendency to a paunch, but as you can see, I don't
know how many years later, I don't have one at all, though of
course that's due to a different remedy, one that is, perhaps, not
exactly to be recommended. And the last few times, when our
friends would drop by as well – there was something both
good and bad about that, don't you think? Of course, it was
more entertaining, and made for rewarding (although occasionally over-long) discussions, which for me always had a
clear purpose: they helped me discover within myself what I
really thought about so many things. But that summer spent
with the others was also bad, because it robbed us of our intimacy and reduced the chances for conversation between the
two of us – to the hours in bed, where we generally employed
other means of communication. And now the clan is scattered
all over the world. Some are no longer with us. I think the
women are in Europe. (Do you write to them?) I understand
that one of the lads is where you are. Do you see him from
time to time? Give him a hug from me. What's he up to? Working? Studying? Is he still such a womanizer? I have fond
memories of his tango expertise and his gifts as a peacemaker.
I wonder what Solís is like these days? And does El Chajá
still exist? It was great to have lunch in that log-walled dining-
room, brimming as usual with English people, as amiable
but distant as ever. Why did the English like that resort so
much? Maybe for the same reasons we did: it was a place
where (at least back then) you could still regain a sense of space;
the beach could be seen as a beach, not one huge shopping
mall, plus sand. The natural surroundings had survived,
because the houses, even the decorously luxurious ones,
weren't blots on the landscape. It was so good to walk and walk

for miles on the shore in the early morning, to feel those gentle little waves on your feet that made you want to go on living. I think we also liked it because in some way it symbolized Uruguay back then, a country of gentle little waves, not the sweeping storms that were to come. There were rocks at one end of the beach, but no crashing waves. You sat down and the water would simply rise in the gaps between the rocks, rushing through and cleansing the little channels, capsizing the crabs and muddling up the half-shells of mussels that would always collect in some corner or other along with the stones and pebbles. Sunset brought with it a different feeling, one that maybe generated less energy, less optimism, but offering instead a tranquillity that I have never felt since. The sun would go down behind the dunes at Jaureguiberry, and the rhythmic, lapping waves would mingle with the occasional lowing of cows that seemed to come from afar, and perhaps because of that sounded taciturn, doom-laden. Some days we caught that fleeting anxiety, but on others it added unexpectedly to how we'd savour the day, simply because we had no real excuse for feeling hypochondriac. Even if your green eyes grew moist and I felt a lump in my throat, we were always aware we had no real reasons to be sad, other than the inherited ones, the ones that come from the mere fact of living and dying. We would walk back slowly, arm in arm and in silence, and in the palm of my right hand I could feel the goose-bumps on the skin of your naked waist, probably because the evening breeze was starting to blow, and we needed to get back to the cabin to put on our pullovers and drink some *grappa* with lemon, and cook the steak with eggs and salad and kiss and nuzzle a bit, not too much, because the best would come later.

Beatriz
(A huge word)

Freedom is a huge word. For example, when classes are over, it's said we're free. As long as you're free, you can walk about, play games, there's no need for you to study. People say a country is free if any woman or man can do as they like there. But even free countries have things that are very forbidden. To kill, for example. Of course, you can kill mosquitoes and cockroaches, and also cattle for steaks. For example, it's forbidden to steal, although it's not serious if you keep some small change when Graciela, who is my mum, sends me on an errand. For example it's forbidden to arrive late at school, although if that happens you have to write a letter, or rather Graciela has to write it, justifying the lateness. That's what the teacher says: *justifying*.

Freedom means many things. For example, if you're not a prisoner, it's said you are free, which means at liberty. But my father is in prison, and yet he is at Liberty, because that's the name of the prison he's been in for many years now. Uncle Rolando says that's an example of irony. One day I told my friend Angélica that the prison my father is in is called Liberty and that Uncle Rolando had said that was an irony and my friend Angélica liked the word so much that when her godfather gave her a puppy she called it Irony. My dad is a prisoner, but not because he has killed or robbed or arrived late at school. Graciela says my dad is at Liberty, in other words, a prisoner, because of his ideas.

It seems my dad was famous for his ideas. I also sometimes have ideas, but I'm not famous yet. That's why I'm not at Liberty, in other words, a prisoner.

If I was a prisoner, I'd like two of my dolls, Toti and Mónica, to be political prisoners as well. I like to fall asleep with at least Toti in my arms. Not so much Mónica, because she is very grumpy. I never hit her, though, to set Graciela a good example.

She has only hit me a few times, but when she does I wish I had loads of freedom. When she hits or scolds me, I call Graciela She, because she doesn't like that. Of course I have to be very angry to call her She. If for example my grandpa comes and asks me, Where is your mother, and I reply, She is in the kitchen, then everyone knows I'm angry, because otherwise I simply say, Graciela is in the kitchen. My grandpa always says I'm the angriest person in the whole family, and that makes me happy. Graciela doesn't much like me calling her Graciela either, but I call her that because it's a pretty name. It's only when I love her very much, when I adore her and kiss and hug her and she says, Ah, little one, don't hug me so hard, that I call her Mother or Mum, and that makes Graciela go all soft and she becomes very tender and strokes my hair, and it wouldn't be like that or so good if I called her Mother or Mummy all the time.

So freedom is a huge word. Graciela says that there's no shame in being a political prisoner like my dad. That it's almost something to be proud of. Why *almost*? Either you are proud or you're ashamed. Would she like me to say I'm almost ashamed? I'm proud, not almost proud, of my dad, because he had loads of ideas, so many that they put him in prison for them. I think that my dad must still have ideas, wonderful ideas, but it's almost certain he doesn't tell anyone about them, because if he does, when he comes out of Liberty to live at liberty, that is, in freedom, they might put him back in Liberty. Do you see how huge the word is?

Exiles
(Penultimate abode)

The death of a comrade (especially when the man in question is some-one so dear to me as Luvis Pedemonte) is always a tearing apart, a rupture. But, when death successfully lays siege in exile, even if it happens in such a fraternal place as this, that rupture has further implications, it takes on another meaning.

Death, that natural conclusion, that obligatory ending, always involves a sense of return. A return to the nourishing homeland; return to the womb of clay, our clay, which will never be the same as any other clay in the world. Death in exile seems like the negation of this return, and is, perhaps, its darkest side.

That's why, during Luvis's prolonged, painful illness, it was so dif-ficult for us to see him light up, enthused, smile, make plans – and even harder for us to keep up the charade, speaking about futures that would include him, imagining or suggesting that he would once more breathe in the air of the streets where he once lived, cast his eyes over the beach, that luminous heart of the day in Montevideo, taste the grapes and peaches, those luxuries of the poor.

How could we talk of the good, simple things that give life in gen-eral its savour and that gave his in particular its very meaning, when we knew that death was on his trail, and that none of us could keep or hide him or die on his behalf, still less call off the pursuing blood-hound, nor even weep tears that might keep him alive, keep him there with us?

In the early days, exile was, among many other things, simply the harsh reality of having to live so far away. Now it is also that of having to die so far away. There are already five or six names on the list. Solitude, sickness or bullets put an end to them, and who knows how many more have now become so many less in this vast, wandering country of ours.

The pill is even bitterer to swallow if we consider that death in exile is evidence that we have all, not just Luvis, but all of us, have all been temporarily robbed of the supreme right to alight from the train at the station where the journey began. They have robbed us of our right to die at home, of a simple death of our own, the death that knows which side we sleep on, what dreams give succour to our waking thoughts.

This is why, when we are forced to concede that Luvis, a comrade cherished like few others, will leave without ever having returned, we promise him that we will fight not only to change life, but also to preserve death, the death that is womb and rebirth, death on and in our own clay.

Luvis was an excellent journalist, a militant revolutionary, a loyal friend and fervent admirer of the Cuban revolution, but possibly we can sum up all his qualities by saying he was an exceptional man of the people, with those attributes of simplicity and modesty, passion and generosity, a great capacity for affection and work, joy and courage, efficiency and responsibility that in some way characterize the best of our people.

In him were to be found two complementary traits that do not always co-exist in an exile. On the one hand, eyes and ears unfailingly attentive to the suffering and struggles, the rumours and images of our distant homeland. On the other, a great ability to be useful, demonstrated in his fruitful integration in Cuba, whose revolution he understood, defended and loved as if it were his own, knowing that, in some way, it was his, it was ours.

With all its frustrations and bitterness, exile never was for him a motive, still less a pretext, for turning inward, for solitude. He knew *that the best remedy for the scourge of exile is integration into the community that receives the exiled person. Inspired by this belief, he worked with determination and joy, almost like a Cuban, while at the same time remaining a whole-hearted Uruguayan.*

We should remind ourselves that among the many clichés of the capitalist world surrounding the business of death, it's often said that it is 'the final abode'. And yet, for a comrade like Luvis, where we are leaving him today will in fact prove to be his penultimate abode, because his final resting place will always be within us, in our affection and memory. And that will be an abode with open doors and windows on to the sky.

Only in this way can we defeat this death, which seems to offer no return. And we will defeat it because no one can doubt that Luvis will return with all those of us who one day go back to our homeland. He will return in our hearts, our minds, our lives. Hearts, minds and lives that will be so much better thanks to the mere fact of returning with such an honest, loyal, such a worthy and generous, such a simple and truthful man of the people.

Battered and Bruised
(Truth and postponement)

Late one afternoon she went to see her father-in-law. She hadn't visited him for about a fortnight. The problem was that their working hours didn't coincide.

'Goodness me,' said Don Rafael, after greeting her with a kiss. 'It must be serious if you've come to visit.'

'Why do you say that? You know very well I like chatting to you.'

'And I like chatting to you. But you only come over when there's a problem.'

'You may be right. I'm sorry.'

'Don't be so ridiculous. Come whenever you like. With or without problems. How's my granddaughter?'

'Come down with a bit of a cold, but in general she's fine. These last few months she's been getting good marks at school.'

'She's clever, but she's canny as well. Let's just say she takes after her grandfather. Was it because of her cold that you didn't bring her?'

'Partly. And also because I wanted to talk to you on my own.'

'I told you so, didn't I? All right, what's the problem?'

Graciela almost flung herself down on the green sofa. She looked slowly and carefully around the slightly untidy room, an old bachelor's apartment. She smiled hesitantly.

'I find it hard to begin. Especially with you. And yet you're the only one I want to talk about this to.'

'Santiago?'

'Yes, or rather, yes and no. The side issue is Santiago, but the main one is me.'

'Ah, how self-obsessed women are.'

'Not just women. But seriously, Rafael, perhaps the real issue is Santiago and me.'

Now her father-in-law sat down, too, in the rocking-chair. His eyes dimmed a little, and he rocked in the chair once or twice before speaking again.

'What isn't working?'

'I'm not working.'

Her father-in-law had apparently decided to get straight to the point.

'You don't love him any more?'

Graciela was obviously not ready to launch into things quite so rapidly. She gave a groan, then blew out her cheeks.

'Stay calm, Graciela.'

'I can't. See how my hands are shaking.'

'If it's of any use to you, I must say I've seen it coming for months. So nothing you say can scare me.'

'You saw it coming? Is it that obvious?'

'No, my girl. It's not that obvious to everyone. But I notice it, purely because I've known you for so many years and besides, I'm Santiago's father.'

On the wall opposite Graciela was a good reproduction of Cezanne's *The Smoker*. She had seen the peaceful image a hundred times, but all of a sudden felt she could no longer bear that gaze, which seemed to be looking askance at her. On other evenings, in other darkened rooms, the Smoker's gaze had seemed to her to be lost in reverie, but now she imagined him staring straight at her. Maybe it was all because of the pipe, which he held in his mouth just the way Santiago did. She averted her eyes and again looked at her father-in-law.

'You must think it's crazy, sheer nonsense. I have to admit that's how it seems to me.'

'At my age nothing seems crazy. You get used to the rejections, the outbursts, the sudden yearnings. Starting with one's own.'

Graciela seemed to take heart. She opened her bag, took out a cigarette and lit it. She offered Don Rafael the packet.

'No thanks. I haven't smoked for six months. Hadn't you noticed?'

'Why did you stop?'

'Circulation problems, but nothing serious. All things considered, it's done me a world of good. It was torture at first, especially after meals. Now I've got used to it.'

Graciela slowly inhaled the smoke, which seemed to lend her courage.

'You asked me if I no longer love Santiago. Whether I answer yes or no, it would be a distortion of the truth.'

'My, things do seem to be getting complicated, don't they?'

'A little. Of course, in one sense I do still love him, amongst other reasons because Santiago has done nothing to make me stop loving him. You know better than anyone how he's behaved. And not merely in terms of his political, militant loyalties. In his personal life, as well. He's always been so good to me.'

'So?'

'So, I still love him as a wonderful friend, a comrade whose behaviour has been beyond reproach. And as the man who in addition is Beatriz's father.'

'But?'

'But as a woman, I don't love him any more. It's in that sense I don't need him, if you follow me.'

'Of course, I understand you. I'm not that stupid. Besides, you've explained very clearly and with a lot of conviction.'

'How can I put it? Perhaps crudely. And I hope you'll forgive me. I don't want to sleep with him any more. That sounds horrible to you, doesn't it?'

'No, it doesn't sound horrible. Sad maybe, but the world hasn't exactly been a *fiesta* lately.'

'If Santiago wasn't in prison, it wouldn't be so serious. It would be simply one of those things that happens to lots of people. We could talk about it, discuss it. I'm sure that in the end Santiago would understand, even if my decision embittered and disillusioned him. But he's in prison.'

'Yes, he's in prison.'

'And that makes me feel trapped, too. He's a prisoner there, but I'm also imprisoned in my situation.'

The phone rang. Graciela pulled a face, annoyed: the ringing spoilt the atmosphere, made it hard to confide. Her father-in-law got up from the rocking-chair and picked up the receiver.

'No, I'm not on my own. But come tomorrow. I'd like to see you. Yes, really. I'm not on my own, but it's not anyone that should worry you. OK, I'll expect you in the evening. How does seven o'clock sound? *Ciao.*'

He hung up and sat down again in the rocking-chair. He glanced at Graciela, weighing up her surprised look. He couldn't help smiling.

'Well, I'm old, but not that old. Besides, complete solitude is a real pain.'

'Yes I must admit I was a bit taken aback, but I'm glad, Rafael. I also feel slightly ashamed. We're always too busy studying our own navels; as though our own problems were the only ones that mattered. We don't always realize that others have theirs, too.'

'Mine isn't what I'd exactly call a problem. She's not a young woman, although she's a lot younger than me. And that's always invigorating. Besides, she's a good person. I still have no idea how long it will last, but for now it does me good. Since we're sharing secrets, I'll confess I feel less insecure now, more optimistic, with a greater desire to go on living.'

'I'm really glad.'

'Yes. And I know you mean that.'

Don Rafael stretched out his arm to a little door in the book-shelves. Opening it, he took out a bottle and two glasses.

'Would you like a drink?'

'Yes, I could do with one.'

Before they drank, they looked at each other in silence. Graciela smiled.

'Your news almost made me forget mine.'

'I don't believe it.'

'I'm joking. How could I forget it?'

'Graciela, is that all there is to it? Not sleeping with Santiago any more, once he eventually gets out of prison? Is that all, or is there something more?'

'There wasn't at first. It was just the growing apart; in reality, *my* growing apart. Coming to rule out any future married life with Santiago.'

'And now?'

'Now it's different. I think I'm starting to fall in love.'

'Ah.'

'I said, I think I'm starting to.'

'Look, if you admit you're starting to, that means you've already fallen in love.'

'That's possible. But I'm not sure. You know him. It's Rolando.'

'How does he feel?'

'It's hard for him as well. He and Santiago were always good friends. Don't think I don't realize this makes things even more complicated.'

'You do make things difficult for yourself, don't you?'

'Tell me about it. Much too difficult.'

'So what are you going to do? Or what have you done already? Have you written to Santiago?'

'That's the main reason I came to see you. I don't know what to do. On the one hand, Santiago keeps writing me tender, loving letters. I know he's sincere. And I feel really phony when I try to reply in the same vein. But then I think it would be awful for him, locked up in Libertad, to get a letter from me one day (I'm sure the military are such sadists that they'd see that he got it straightaway), telling him not only that I don't want to be his wife any more, but, to make it even worse, that I'm in love with one of his best friends. Some days I understand that in spite of everything it's best for me to tell him and get it over with; on others I feel that it would be unnecessarily cruel.'

'Painful, isn't it?'

'Yes.'

'I'm inclined to think that the mere fact of telling him would be what you've just said: unnecessarily cruel. You and Beatriz are Santiago's reasons for staying alive.'

'What about you?'

'I'm his father. That's different. Our parents are given to us; no one chooses them. But it takes an act of will, you take a conscious decision to choose a wife and to have children. Obviously, Santiago loves me and I love him, but there's always been a certain distance between us. It was different with his mother. She managed to talk to him, really get through to him, and for Santiago her death was a catastrophe; it was hard for him to come to terms with. Of course it was, he was only fifteen at the time. But as I was saying, now, and with him being where he is, you and Beatriz are his future; whether in the medium or long term doesn't matter. He thinks that some-day he'll rejoin you two and everything will begin again.'

'Yes, that's what he thinks.'

'Well, as you say, if he weren't in prison all this would be sad, but more normal. For a couple to break up is never a good thing, but sometimes to carry on under false pretences can be much worse.'

'So, what do you advise, Rafael?'

Don Rafael raises his glass and downs the whisky he had poured himself. Now he's the one to puff out his cheeks.

'It's always risky, getting mixed up in other people's lives.'

'But Santiago is your son.'

'And you're like a daughter to me.'

'That's how I feel, too.'

'I know. Which is why it's even more complicated.'

The phone rings again, but this time her father-in-law doesn't pick up.

'Don't worry, it's not Lydia. Did I tell you her name? The person who always calls at this hour is a real pain. A student who asks me interminable questions about bibliography.'

Apparently, the student is insistent or stubborn or both, because the phone carries on ringing. Finally, silence returns.

'Since you're asking, I'd be in favour of you not writing any-thing about it. You should go on pretending. I know that makes you feel bad. But remember, you are free. You have other objects of interest and affection, whereas all he has are four walls and a barred window. Telling him the truth would des-troy him. And I don't want my son to be destroyed now, not when he has survived so many calamities. Someday, when he's out (and I know he is going to get out), you'll be able to tell him everything, and come face to face with his bitterness. And when that occasion arises, I authorize you to tell him that I was the one who advised you to stay silent. At first, he'll be really angry, he'll explode like he used to in the good old days, he may even weep, and think the world is collapsing. But by then he'll no longer be enclosed within four walls, he'll be far from the bars, like you, he'll have other objects of interest and affection. Well, that's my opinion. You asked for it.'

'Yes, I asked you for it.'

'So what do you think?'

Now her father-in-law seemed more anxious and nervous than she was. When he tilted the bottle again, he noticed that his hand holding the glass was trembling slightly. Graciela saw it, too.

'Calm down,' she said, parodying him. He relaxed and laughed reluctantly. 'Perhaps it's for the best. Or at least, it's the only sensible course.'

'I understand that no solution is entirely acceptable. And do you know why not? Because the only truly unacceptable thing is what Santiago is going through.'

'I think I'll follow your advice. I'll go on pretending.'

'Besides, the future may hold surprises. For everyone. Although you don't need him today, you might need him again.'

'You think I'm fickle, don't you, Rafael?'

'No. I think that all of us, those here and those elsewhere, are all out of kilter. We do as best we can to organize ourselves, to start over, to sort out our feelings, our relationships, our nostalgias. But as soon as we let things slip, chaos resurfaces. And each new lapse into chaos (sorry for repeating myself) is increasingly chaotic.'

Graciela closed her eyes for a moment. Intrigued, her father-in-law peered at her, possibly afraid she might burst into tears. But when she opened her eyes once more, they were only slightly moist, or perhaps a little shiny. She stared down at the empty glass still in her hand, and held it out to Don Rafael.

'Can I have another?'

Don Rafael
(News of Emilio)

I feel as though I've been crushed, as if I'm lost. As if I'm gasp-
ing for breath, but without panting. As if after a wretched,
tough lesson of what being a father means. As if I were seeing
myself from a distance in a shop window, and my image was
that of a mannequin made all the more ridiculous because all it
was wearing was a tie. Fortunately, it seems I convinced Graciela, but am I myself convinced? Hypocrisy may be a vice, but
I'm not so sure that frankness is always a virtue. I want to be
realistic, I want to be broad-minded, I want to be flexible, I
want to be up to date. The trouble is that I'm also a father. In
other words, when, finally, Santiago gets out of prison (the lawyer has just sent me a fairly hopeful letter) a different woman
will be waiting for him. He will have to see Graciela through
the bars of another man's love. To collect Beatriz at weekends
and take her to the zoo and parks and occasionally to the movies. To ask her as few awkward questions as possible, because
her every reply, however innocent she may be, is bound to
upset him, or lead him to speculate. And how is he going to
deal with Rolando? As his former comrade, one he even shared
a cell with, or as the man who is sleeping with his wife? What's
going on with my son, gentlemen? I know what his qualities
are, and even what he had too much of, but the question today
is about what he lacks. What's missing in this story? I've no problem imagining the ins and outs that lead people to love him,

but confess I'm at a loss to identify the things that bring about this loss of love. What shortcomings has he inherited from me, from his mother? I have to find out. I have to unearth the real son, whom I perhaps don't even know as yet. Precisely today I dusted off the clandestine letter, the only one that so far (I still have no idea by what strange channel) he was able to send me with complete certainty that it wouldn't pass through the prison censors. And strangely, the letter was sent to me, and not Graciela:

Just think, Dad, how sure I must be that *this* mail is secure for me to decide to tell you of the indiscretions you're just about to read. I have to send signals to someone from this wilderness, and who else could it be but you? I have to send signals so as not to go to pieces, not to fall apart. Don't worry, it's only a figure of speech. But, in some way, it translates a feeling, doesn't it? Let's be clear: don't be afraid that I've talked, or given someone away. Not that. You taught me a few things, and that's one lesson I did learn. Oh, but I'm not a hero either. Would you be astonished if I told you I'm still not sure if I stayed silent out of conviction or self-interest? Yes, self-interest. I always noticed that if you deny everything, if you persist in saying No and No again with your head, hands, lips, eyes and throat, those people still use you as a punchbag of course, but just occasionally you notice that deep down they suspect you're telling the truth; in other words, that you know absolutely nothing. If on the other hand you weaken and say the slightest thing, a trifle that maybe is of no use to them at all and which doesn't hurt anyone, then their attitude changes, because from that moment on they do think you know a whole lot more, and really go for you, they tear you apart. If you consistently deny everything, of course they're going to smash you up, but it's also possible that one day they may leave you in peace, because they're convinced it's true that you don't know a thing. But if you say something, even the tiniest detail, then they'll never leave you alone. Perhaps they might lay off you for a while, but soon they'll return to the charge. They're obsessed with getting the rest of it out of you. That's why, I repeat, I'm not sure if I stayed silent out of conviction or self-interest. Maybe the latter. But in the end, those are defences you put up. At any rate, I'm fine with it, as no one was caught just because I caved in at some point or other. But that's not what I want to talk to you about. You know what the lawyer's argument has always been: that I didn't kill anyone. Remember that? But I did. Don't have a heart attack, will you? Neither the lawyer, nor my comrades, Graciela nor anybody else knows about this. You're the only one who's hearing it, and that's because I just have to get it off my chest. You can see what a huge risk I'm running by putting it down here in black and white, and yet I'm doing so because I cannot bear the weight of it alone any longer. I'll tell you what happened. For about ten days I'd been in the hideout – one of many. I'd spent the last two of them all on my own, without ever going outside, eating only from tins, reading thrillers, listening to the transistor radio with earpieces in to avoid attracting attention. The shutters were closed all day. At night, too, of course, but I never turned a light on. We had to give the impression the house was empty. The big advantage of that particular hideout was that it had exits to two different streets, which, despite everything, gave me some security, because the second exit was well concealed: at the end of a corridor with flats on either side. Most of them were bachelor pads, so there weren't many people around, which also helped. I always slept with one eye open, and one night some slight noises and almost imperceptible footsteps made me open the other one as well. It seemed as if the sounds were coming from the small front garden. I looked through the shutters and saw a slightly swaying shadow, though I couldn't tell if it was of a man or a dwarf pine planted in the flowerbed. I didn't move, but, all of a sudden, I sensed someone was prowling around inside the house. Thinking it over now, I reckon they were so sure no one was there they'd relaxed their normal security measures. Besides, I guess there were only a few of them, three or four, and that they had approached the house not because they knew anything definite, but because by that point they were suspicious of everything. Suddenly I was caught in the beam of a torch. A minute went by that seemed like an eternity to me, then a voice whispered: 'Santiago, what are you doing here?' At first, I thought it must be a comrade, but it couldn't have been, because they all knew me by another name. When the figure shifted the beam of his torch away slightly, I saw his uniform first of all, then the weapon he was brandishing, and finally, his face. Do you know who it was? Hold on tight, Dad. It was Emilio. Yes, the very same, the one you're thinking of, Aunt Ana's son, your nephew. You can't imagine the images that flash through your mind at a time like that. I had little scope to make decisions; he was the one in charge of the situation, because I had no chance of reaching my revolver. There were footsteps, more noises in the little garden. He spoke again: 'Give yourself up, Santiago. It's for the best – I didn't know you were mixed up in this, give yourself up.' And he stared at the gun, not his, but mine, the one I couldn't reach. 'I didn't know you were mixed up in this either, Emilio.' We were both whispering. 'So many years since we last saw each other,' he murmured. 'Not a good moment to meet again, is it?' I whispered. And I made a snap decision. I joined my fists together and went up to him, as if to let him handcuff me – 'All right, I surrender.' And he trusted me. He wouldn't have trusted anyone else. He let me approach; I think he even lowered his gun a little. I don't know now what speedy movements I made, but the fact is that three seconds later, instead of being forced into cuffs, these hands of mine were squeezing his neck, and went on squeezing until he stopped moving. I don't know how it could all have happened so silently. The shadows of other figures were still moving out in the garden, but they weren't speaking: obviously, they didn't want to give their presence away. I was barefoot, but dressed; I always slept with my clothes on. I walked as quickly as I could towards the second exit, picking up a pair of rope sandals from a chair on my way. I reached the door to the other street, the one that gave on to the line of studios. There were no shutters or spyholes on that side, so I simply had to take a risk, and I did. I went out and no one was there. It was three in the morning. I advanced all of ten metres, trying not to run, and then, suddenly, I saw it. I couldn't believe my eyes: a bus was coming slowly along, with only two passengers on board – one of those old Cutcsa buses with an open platform. I leapt on it. Half an hour later, I got off in Plaza Independencia. The newspapers never mentioned that failed mini-operation, and Emilio's name never appeared as one of the noble victims of murderous subversion. There was only the funeral notice. And we (you, me, Graciela) were among the relatives expressing their profound grief at his death. Maybe you even went to the vigil. I didn't, obviously, although for a moment I was tempted to. But by then I was really on the run. A year later, when they captured us in the raid on Villa Muñoz, they interrogated me hundreds of times, they took me to pieces, but they never asked me about that particular event. Why didn't they ever mention it? I'll never know. The fact is, nobody in the family knew Emilio was a cop. But if his profession was such a mystery, why was he wearing a uniform? You must be asking why I'm loading all this on to you. I'm telling you because I've never managed to free myself of that act, which I was cornered into. Petty-bourgeois prejudice on my part? Possibly. Ironically, it's the only time I have killed. I've been in more than one shootout and several times was on the brink of being snuffed out, I've been on the point of finishing someone else off, but it seems my aim leaves a lot to be desired. I have no other deaths to my credit (or should that be debit?). So, what's the problem? The thing is, I can't forget my cousin's face. Or forget my hands strangling him. Two or three times a month I dream of Emilio, but never in the act of killing him. They're not nightmares.

I dream of a very distant past, when we were both young boys (he was a year older than me, wasn't he?), and we used to play football in the little field behind the church, or when, during the summer months, we went to the Prado at siesta-time, while you adults had to take a nap and we felt especially free. We stretched out on the grass or the mattresses of leaves, and fantasized, made plans in which we were going to be together and travel, always by boat – because we were scared of planes and besides, as Emilio used to say, on the ship's deck we could play leapfrog and jacks, whereas the air hostesses banned that on planes. We went on fantasizing: he was going to be an engineer, because I like mathematics, he used to say, and I was going to be a musician, because I liked to play *La Cumparsita* by blowing on a comb with a cigarette paper folded round it. We also talked about you grown-ups, and he was always adamant: They don't understand us, but they do love us, and we set an age limit of fourteen for us to escape, once and for all, from his house and mine, and so begin the tale of adventures we had so often spoken of. That's the Emilio I dream about, and that's why they're not nightmares. The nightmare comes when I wake up and see my hands squeezing his throat, which wasn't soft and narrow, like when we were eight, nine or ten, but short and thick; or maybe that's how it seemed to me because of the collar of his uniform. His name has been mentioned several times here in prison, or before that in the barracks. Nobody knew he was my cousin, but they all agreed he was a butcher, one of the most savage torturers, a rat who enjoyed sticking the electric prod up the prisoners' arses or on their balls. Some of them are aware he died a while ago, but don't know the circumstances. I don't say a word when somebody remarks, I hope he didn't die a natural death, I hope they smashed that bastard's skull, the shitty sadist, and other equally appreciative terms. So, it's not exactly a sense of guilt that disturbs me, but rather the thought that in those early hours I somehow strangled my childhood. And maybe the memory of the look of trust he had when I brought my hands together as if I wanted him to handcuff me. And today, when I think about what, back then, his reason for whispering might have been. Perhaps because he thought I wasn't alone in the house and so wasn't sure of his position, even though he realized I couldn't reach my gun. Or maybe it was so that the others didn't kill me out of sheer nervousness, or pure cruelty, because, after all, I was his cousin Santiago and it was better to have me surrender alive and not to take me down as a corpse, running the risk that someday the family might discover what a huge mess it had been. Or perhaps because he also suddenly remembered all our shared past, with our fantasies on the grass and the mattresses of leaves, and that disconcerted him and left him defenceless. Or perhaps he was not struck as quickly as I was by the profound ideological differences pitting us against one another, in a desperate struggle where being cousins counted for nothing. But I had never killed anyone, Dad, and I think that this, my one experience of it, has marked me for ever. That might mean that I'm a coward, even though I've been very strong in other ways. And I have to add that I don't think I would feel the same if I had killed him in a shootout. I feel like this because I killed him in that way – an ignoble way, perhaps underhand, using and abusing his surprise, that was (if I'm honest, I'm sure it was) an affectionate surprise. And even though I now know he had turned into a really sinister character, a bloodthirsty sort with no scruples, and everybody says, me included, that he's better off dead, the fact is that when I grabbed his neck with my clawing hands I didn't know any of that: I killed him purely and simply to survive. I killed the person who had dreamed longside me and with whom I had made plans to escape from his house and mine, dreams of trips on boats, playing jacks and leapfrog. They are – how can I put it? – two different sets of values, two distinct identities, two juxtaposed Emilios. Can you understand that, Dad? I'm not telling Graciela and I never will, because she wouldn't understand, because she always sees things in black or white. She could say, You did well, that's one butcher less. Or she could say: How could you do that to your cousin? But it's neither one thing nor the other. It's more complicated, Dad, more complicated. Now here's a thing. Bear in mind that this letter is a unique opportunity (I hope one day I'll be able to tell you how this incredible chance came about), which I'm sure will never be repeated. It's impossible for you to reply to me through the same channel or any other that is as trustworthy. And yet you must send me a reply. Isn't that right: You will reply, won't you? You'll have to do it in the normal way, the one that is bound to go through prison censorship. You'll have to limit yourself to one of two alternative replies, even though we both know how many gradations might lie between them. Take note, then. If you can identify with the situation – I'm not saying if you approve of it or can justify it, but if, at least, you comprehend it – find a way so that, two lines before you sign off, the word 'understand' appears. If, on the other hand, it seems to you something that is abject or inadmissible, then put 'I don't understand'. Agreed? *Ciao*, Dad.

I read that letter about ten times and it took me two days before I could begin to write back to him. My letter ended like this: 'As pretty and smart as ever, my granddaughter, who, less importantly, is also your daughter, has begun to learn French: what do you make of that? Sometimes when she comes to see me she brings me up to date with her latest Froggie lesson. But I must be a bit hard of hearing (ah, the years don't pass in vain) or perhaps it's my memory, but I can barely understand her when she tells me, in her polished Alliance Française accent, one of Perrault's fairy stories. *Ciao*, my son.'

The Other
(Flabbergasted and everything)

It's a new sensation for him. It's not unpleasant, far from it. But the fact is, he's got himself into a right mess. This has never happened to him before, with any woman. He, Rolando Asuero, was the one who took the initiative, was in charge of every relationship, whether or not it ended up in bed. And it was a matter of principle: it would always be temporary, with every fact and intention out in the open, as transparent as H_2O, so that nobody could accuse him later of unfulfilled promises, holding his word against him. As Ecclesiastes neglected to say: In order not to break promises, it's best not to make them in the first place. Fortunately, as he has to admit, he had always met understanding and willing women, who from the moment of kick-off accepted the rules of the game and who afterwards, when the final whistle blew, made themselves scarce with a friendly 'So long, it's been good to know you.' Besides, he had always treated the owners or slaves (well, actually, the wives) of his closest friends as sisters, and if on occasion he had given them the odd incestuous glance, he never crossed the good-humoured, comradely boundary, even if he often aroused their innate coquettishness. Incestuous glances which, in the past, had not infrequently been directed at Graciela, when, in Solís, that rough and ready seaside resort, she had put on her flimsy blue two-piece swimsuit (not a bikini, the Apostle Santiago's cautious liberalism having not yet extended that far), which revealed her figure, or *habeas corpus*, truly worthy of consideration, of fantasy, ah but he had never gone beyond the modest limit of a sigh or shameless gazes of admiration from behind his dark glasses, occasionally even encouraged by some comment or other from Santiago himself, who, seeing her skipping through the waves one afternoon like a woman in a TV advert, let's say, would murmur to himself (but in reality for the benefit of the other three), That skinny ribs is beautiful, isn't she?, leading to banter and macho chuckles, well, macho in a manner of speaking, from the other two husbands and the confirmed bachelor, namely he, Rolando Asuero, at your service and also at the service of your good lady wife. An infamous and in no way innocent remark he had once addressed, a decade earlier, to the general manager of a big company who had decided on the spot to demote him to an ex-cashier.

But today's Graciela is something else. And he, too, has changed. How could he not? First came the political phase, with those two years before the coup that were quite simply hellish. So, what happens to the erotic in such moments? A pithy question for the Sphinx, Anwar el-Sadat's laconic great-grandmother. Ah, but how difficult it is to be erotic in a time of desperate clandestine activity. During those two ferocious years, sometimes you couldn't even find a camp bed to sleep on, let alone have time for any other activities. And then the damned cops, with their episodes of interrogation, cattle prods, waterboarding and other delights. Of course, in those days, your noggin could never stop working overtime. You accept the limitations, of course you do, and afterwards you don't even remember, because at night, when not even the cockroach appears to watch over you, you bury your head in that excuse for a pillow and cry your eyes out until you're dehydrated from so many tears (TH, in other words, *tango habemus*: 'Crazy in my sadness', ah but never, 'How weak I was, how blind'.) Yes, today's

Graciela is very different. Firstly, she has matured, become more of a woman; but secondly, she has grown less sure of herself, perhaps because of that very maturity. In body (and soul, too, let's not be dogmatic), she has matured remarkably, spectacularly, and to watch her, for example, slowly making her way up between the flowerbeds to her apartment building (where he, so often, would be waiting in the doorway) stirs great – though not often realized – expectations. It's true she's unsure of herself, disconcerted, although, maybe, it would be more correct to say 'disoriented'. And the eye of the storm: Santiago. Santiago in prison, neither able to attack nor to defend himself, all alone with his blues and his cultural heritage, what terminology, eh, but also what a *situacão*! Rolando has come to a preliminary diagnosis: Graciela is a girl who can't get used to distance, and that is where, willy-nilly, poor Santiago has lost out. But he is still a long way from even beginning to imagine that he, Rolando Asuero, has a role to play in this story. He doesn't know. Not yet. Although he's coming to know. He likes Graciela, there's no point underplaying or contesting that. And he admits that, on various occasions, when she talked to him about the cobwebs in her attic, or her changeable moods, her highs and lows, he had made wary advances, made suggestive hints, had offered, let's say, fraternal support, and little by little, maybe without even intending to, had let slip veiled but unambiguous allusions to a certain fond interest in her, or rather, to the attraction he felt for her. And obviously, in her insecure state, with her constantly revising and rejecting each sensation, each emotion, Graciela soaked things up like a Grecian sponge. And she must have sensed his cautious, discreet manoeuvring. Then one day all of a sudden, in the midst of one of those ambiguous, tightrope-walking conversations, she blurted out: I don't need Santiago any more, he abandoned me, to which he, Rolando, had replied sympathetically, No,

Graciela, he didn't abandon you, he was taken from you, and her reply, I know, that's why I say it's absurd, absurd, or perhaps in exile I've been transformed into somebody else, and so he had said, Perhaps you don't share Santiago's political beliefs any longer, and her, Of course I do, they're mine as well, and so he, at last, asked the million-dollar question, Do you dream of other men, and she had said, Do you mean dream in my sleep or daydreams, and he, Both, and she, When I sleep I don't dream of any man, and he, What about when you're awake? And she, well, awake, yes, I do daydream and you're going to laugh, and there she paused, not a theatrical pause, but simply a short silence to take a breath, to feel the weight of what she was about to add: I dream of you. He had been flabbergasted, had felt a sudden rushing sound in his ears, a fine Don Juan he was, actually he had bit his lip until it bled, although he didn't realize it until hours later. And she, tense opposite him, waiting for something, not knowing exactly what, but tremendously insecure, because among other things, she was imagining he must be torturing himself at that moment over the word 'loyalty', loyalty to his friend all alone in his cell, which even if it was clean was still disgusting; loyalty to a heavy, well worn past and a morality never made explicit but nonetheless real, and to the endless discussions into the early hours, with Silvio (who's no longer here), too, and Manolo, now an electronics technician in Gothenburg, and their wives, semi-marginalized by the macho-Leninism of the illustrious males, but occasionally joining in with obvious objections, but more than anything preparing salads-steaks-*gnocchi-empanadas-escalopes*-caramel-jam and then washing-up while the men were flat out in their siestas. He had been flabbergasted, him such a Casanova and whoremonger, his face bathed in sweat like a schoolboy seduced by a chorus girl, and with an itch in his left ankle that was probably an allergic reaction to the stormy future approaching. Flabbergasted and everything, he had managed to stammer, Gra-graciela, don't p-play with fire, and had even tried to steer the conversation in a more light-hearted direction, with something like, The flesh is weak and thou shalt not covet thy neighbour's wife, all to give himself the tiniest respite, ah but she kept her startlingly grave expression, Look I'm not joking, this is too serious for me, so he, I'm sorry, Graciela, it's the shock, don't you see, and after this sentence straight out of a Buenos Aires farce he no longer stammered and no longer felt flabbergasted, but well and truly astounded, and yet was able to mutter, It's a shame I can't tell you not to talk nonsense, because I can see in your eyes that you're talking terribly seriously, and It's also a shame I can't tell you, Look, I can't do this, because I can. And as soon as he said that 'I can', he felt he had been sincere and fateful – sincere because that truly was the safari feeling that was starting to push its way through the tiny jungle of his astonishment, and fateful because it did not escape him that this relatively rash 'I can' was something like the first sign of his personal apocalypse. But now it had been said and underlined, and Graciela, who had been prettily pale, suddenly blushed and sighed like someone going into a high-class florist's, and he thought now it was time to stretch out a hand and so he extended it over the coffee table cleverly avoiding the vase with no carnations and the ashtray full of butts and for a while, let's say four seconds, she hesitated and then also held out her slender hand that looked like a pianist's, but was in fact a typist's, and this became the acid test because in the end the contact with each other's hand was sufficiently revealing and they looked at each other as if discovering one another. After that came the lengthy analysis, once more the word 'loyalty' had leapt over the vase with no flowers and the ashtrays full of butts, alighting now on his rough knuckles, now on her fragrant neckline, and Graciela, for now, more tormented than happy, I know it's unjust, but at this stage of the game I can't lie to myself and I know only too well what I owe Santiago, but obviously that conviction does not insure us against marital estrangement and Rolando on his side, for now more disconcerted than happy, Let's take this slowly, Let's take it as if Santiago were here right now, listening to our conversation, because he's an inescapable part of this situation, Let's take it as if Santiago could really understand and above all first understanding it ourselves. And they talked and smoked like this for a couple of hours, almost without touching each other, discussing solutions and resolutions, very warily bringing up the question of Beatriz, not yet daring to scrutinize or plan the future, promising to give themselves time to get used to the idea, also promising themselves not to do anything too crazy, or anything too sensible, and Rolando feeling increasingly hypnotized by her superb green eyes and her legs and her waist, and Graciela evidently disturbed by his reaction, which nevertheless she wanted and was waiting for, and Rolando starting to fall in love with that anxiousness and Graciela suddenly sliding defenceless into a fit of sobbing that was unpremeditated and therefore all the more persuasive, and he taking her face in both hands and only then realizing, when he made gentle contact with her lips, that out of pure astonishment he had bitten his own a few hours earlier when she had said, I dream of you.

Beatriz
(Pollution)

Uncle Rolando said this city is becoming godawful because of all the pollution. I didn't say anything, so I wouldn't seem stupid, but the only word I understood was 'city'. I looked in the dictionary, but 'godawful' isn't there. On Sunday when I went to visit Grandpa I asked him what 'godawful' means. He laughed and explained very politely that it meant 'unbearable'. I understood the meaning of that because Graciela, that is my mum, occasionally says to me (or rather almost every day), Please, Beatriz, sometimes you can be really unbearable. Precisely that Sunday evening she told me so, although she repeated please please please three times, Beatriz, sometimes you are just unbearable, so I very calmly said, You probably meant to say godawful, which she thought was funny, not hilarious, but enough for her to stop my punishment (which was very important). That other word, 'pollution', is more difficult. That word is in the dictionary. It says: 'pollution': *emission of semen*. What can 'emission' and 'semen' mean? I looked the first one up and it says: 'emission': *an issuing of something*. I also looked for 'semen', and it says: *seed, liquid that serves for reproduction*. So what Uncle Rolando meant is: this city is becoming unbearable from so much issuing of semen. I didn't understand that either, and so the next time I met my friend Rosita I explained the serious problem I had and what the dictionary said. She said: I get the impression that semen is a sensual word, but I don't know what it means. She promised me she would consult her cousin Sandra, because she's older and in her school they have sensual education classes. On Thursday Rosita came to visit me, very mysterious, I know her well, and when she's being mysterious she wrinkles up her nose. Graciela was at home and so she waited very patiently for her to go into the kitchen to prepare the *escalopes* and then told me, I've found out, semen is something that grown-up men have, not boys, so I said, So we don't have semen yet, and she said, Don't be silly not now or ever, only men have semen when they're old like my dad or your dad who's in prison, girls don't have semen, not even when we're grannies, and I said, How strange, and she said, Sandra says that all boys and girls come from semen because the liquid has little creatures in it called spermatozoids and Sandra was pleased because in yesterday's class they had learned that spermatozoid is written with a z. After Rosita went home I was left thinking, and it seemed to me Uncle Rolando perhaps meant to say that the city was unbearable because it had so many spermatozoids (with a z) in it. So I went to see Grandpa again, because he always helps me, but not too much, and when I told him what Uncle Rolando had said and asked him if it was true that the city was becoming godawful because it had so many spermatozoids in it, he laughed so much he almost choked and I had to fetch him a glass of water, and he went very red and I was scared he might have a fit with me all on my own in such an unbearable situation. Luckily, he calmed down little by little, and when he could speak again he told me, still coughing, that what Uncle Rolando had said referred to was 'almospheric' contamination. I felt even more of a fool, but then he explained that the almosphere was the air and because in this city there are loads of factories and automobiles, all that smoke dirties the air, that is the almosphere, and that is the rotten pollution and not semen like the dictionary says, and we shouldn't breathe it in, but if we don't breathe we die anyway, so there's nothing for it but to breathe in all that mess. I told Grandpa that now I realized that my dad had at least a small advantage where he's a prisoner, because it's a place where there aren't many factories or automobiles because the prisoners' families are poor and don't have automobiles. And Grandpa said, Yes, I was right, and that we should always look for the positive side of things. So I gave him a big kiss and his beard prickled me more than usual, and I went running to look for Rosita and as her mum was there, whose name is Asunción, just like the capital of Paraguay, the two of us waited very patiently until finally she went to water the plants and then I said, very mysterious, You can tell your cousin Sandra from me that she's much sillier than we are, because I've looked into it all and we don't come from semen, but from the almosphere.

Exiles

(The acoustics at Epidaurus)

> *If there is a sound at Epidaurus*
> *It can be heard up at the top, among the trees,*
> *In the air.*
>
> Roberto Fernández Retamar

We were in epidaurus twenty-five years after roberto
And also heard from the topmost rows
The scrape of a match that down below
Was lit by our guide the same little plump woman
Who between temple and mausoleum
Between an ounce of socrates and a drop of thermopylae
Had told us how niarchos managed to
Pay no more than nine thousand drachmas
That is about three hundred dollars of tax a year
And in her youthful enthusiasm had announced
To the astonishment of five tourists from buenos aires
Experts in tato bores[*] quotes
The upcoming and completely certain victory of the socialist
    papandreu
So we were in epidaurus breathing the transparent dry air
And contemplating the profuse immemorial greens

---

* Tato Bores: An Argentine comedian famous in the 1970s and 1980s.

Of the trees that turned and turn their backs on the theatre
And their faces to the pale hollow
Greens and air probably not so different from
Those polycleitus the younger contemplated and breathed
When he was doing his calculations of eternity and enigma
And I too went down to the magical centre of the orchestra
So that luz could take the obligatory photo
In this place of such popular and solid memory
And from there I wanted to test the extraordinary acoustics
And thought hello líber hello héctor hello raúl hello jaime*
Very slowly like someone striking a match or crumpling a
    ticket
And so I could confirm how excellent the acoustics were
Because my secretive greetings could be heard not only on the
    terraces
But high in the sky with a single bird
And they crossed the peloponnese the ionic and tyrrhenian
    seas
The mediterranean the atlantic and nostalgia
And finally slid between the bars
Like a transparent dry breeze

* Political prisoners under the Uruguayan dictatorship: Líber Seregni, Héctor Rodríguez, Raúl Sendic, Jaime Pérez.

Intramural
(A mere possibility)

Yesterday the lawyer came and gave me to understand that things are looking more hopeful. That it's not impossible. That it's possible. A mere possibility, I know. But I have to admit, it shocked me, I think my heart even started pounding. Not that I ever gave up hope. I always knew that one day I would meet you all again. But it's one thing to imagine that an indefinite number of years have to go by before it happens, and very different when the prospect suddenly comes within the realm of the possible. I don't want to get my hopes up. And yet I can't help it. And that's understandable, don't you think? It was only the day before yesterday that I thought it likely I would be in here for many years to come, I'd even mentally prepared myself to get used to paying this tax, 'to kiss the lash' as that priest from Salto with the diabolical voice used to say, if you remember? Now though, when the possibility arises that perhaps, maybe, just maybe, that potentially it might be only a year now, or even less, it's curious, but this period of time which is so definite – well, it's somehow even more unbearable than that other indefinite, almost infinite period I had managed to resign myself to. We're complicated creatures, aren't we? And you and Dad, what do you think? Don't say anything to Beatriz yet, we don't want her to get her hopes up and then have her find they come to nothing; at her age that could be really damaging. The mere thought that I might see her soon, let's say in a quantifiable length of time, gives me gooseflesh. To see you, and Dad, that's another matter. You can imagine how much I want to look at you, to hug you. To talk and talk with you both, my God, that'll be a real treat. But the thought of Beatriz sets me on edge. Five years without seeing a child, especially when she is so young, is an eternity. Five years without seeing an adult, however much you love them, are simply five years, even though that is tremendous, too. For example, you'll find I have absolutely no paunch, and less hair (I'm not talking about the obvious work of the in-house hairdresser – it's clearly receding in a way that has nothing to do with the orthodoxy here). I've lost a few incisors and molars, too (don't panic – I didn't write *morals*!) What else? Well, a few new freckles, birthmarks, one or two scars. As you can see, I know myself inside out. The thing is, in the kind of situation I find myself in, austere as a monastery, one's own body inevitably becomes all-important. And that's not down to any narcissism, it's just because, for hour after hour, there are no other signs of life anywhere near. For my part, I know the old man will have quite a few more grey hairs. Not more wrinkles, though, because that old gypsy was born wrinkled. I remember when I was little I was always impressed by the wrinkles and lines he had around his eyes, and on his forehead. Apparently, that never stopped him hitting the jackpot with the ladies. I think that even when the old lady was alive he was still quite a flirt. And how will I find you? More mature, obviously, and therefore more beautiful. Sometimes the anxieties of the past leave a bitter grimace on a face; at least, that's what the turn-of-the-century novelists used to write. Nowadays they don't employ such corny turns of phrase, even though grimaces haven't gone out of style, and bitterness is still as rife. But I know you don't have that kind of grimace, and if you do, it doesn't matter, I'll cure you of it. Yes, you're probably more serious, you won't laugh as gaily, in the same spring-like way as you used to. But there's also no doubt you will have retained and enriched your capacity for happiness, your vocation for making the very best of things. If what the lawyer suggested does in fact end up happening, I haven't the faintest idea of how (and if) I'll be able to join you. I mean: I don't know whether they'll let me leave the country. I know only too well that as far as that goes everything will be complicated, but it's bound to be better than the present separation, which, right now, well, I can't decide whether it's unjust, absurd, or deserved. I'd prefer to travel, of course, because what's left of my family here? Following Emilio's death, there's only Aunt Ana, but I don't think I really want to see her; after all, she has never tried to visit me. They say she's even frailer these days, that must be why. As for my other cousins, for obvious reasons, they can't come to see me, and even if I do get out, I don't think I could see them. To find work here would be very difficult, for all sorts of reasons, which is why I insist it would be best for me to travel, but it's too soon to speculate about that (simply on the basis of the scanty information I have, it's merely been hinted at by the lawyer) in any detail. Meanwhile, I think. About specific things. Faced with this new possibility, all of a sudden, I've stopped fantasizing, taking refuge in memories, reconstructing episodes from Solís or in our house, seeing shapes and faces in the damp patches on the walls. Now I'm focusing on concrete matters: work, studies, family life, all kinds of projects. It wouldn't be a bad idea to complete my studies. Why don't you try to find out at the university there what subjects they would recognize and which ones I'd have to retake? Just in case. And work? I know you have a good job, but I want to work as soon as possible. And don't think that's just machismo. You have to understand that all my life I've worked and studied at the same time, so I've grown used to it, and even to like it. Why don't you and Dad start looking into that? You two know what I can do best, but with things as they are I'm not going to expect that any job will correspond exactly to my knowledge or vocation. I'm prepared to do anything, you understand: anything. Physically, I've nearly recovered, and I'm sure that there I'll get completely better: always being careful, obviously, not to let my paunch spread again. My mouth starts watering as soon as I imagine I could have a normal life again, a life with you, Beatriz and Dad. For a fortnight now, I've had somebody to share my space with, my roommate, let's say. He's a great guy, we get on magnificently. And yet I don't dare talk to him about this new possibility, simply because he doesn't have it, not for now, at least, and if I give full rein to my euphoria (always with the intimate and inevitable suspicion I might be suffering from acute *optimatitis*), I'm afraid I might cause him, even indirectly, despair and sorrow. We are all generous, or at least we've learned to be so, in here, especially once the first stage is behind us, during which, of course, we are selfish, inward-looking, grim, even hypochondriacal; but generosity also has its limits, its territory and its impossibilities. I remember very clearly that a little more than a year ago, when J. got out, I myself had conflicting feelings. How could I not be pleased that someone like him, an exceptional guy, would be reunited with his wife and mother and able to work again and feel himself to be a complete human being? Yet his absence was also disheartening, first and foremost because J. was a wonderful person to share the twenty-four hours with, and secondly because his departure revealed to me how tough and sad it was, my having to stay behind. It's odd, but good companionship doesn't always mean talking or listening, sharing lives and deaths, loves and failures in love, telling each other the plots of novels we read long ago and no longer have with us, discussing philosophy and its offshoots, drawing conclusions from past experiences, analysing and re-analysing ourselves ideologically, exchanging tales of our respective childhoods or, whenever possible, playing chess. Often, real companionship consists in remaining silent, respecting the other person's inability to speak, understanding that this is what he needs on this particular dark day, and then supporting him with our own silence, or allowing him to do the same for us, but, and this *but* is fundamental, without either of the two of us asking for it or demanding it, simply that the other person understands it for himself, in spontaneous solidarity. Sometimes, a good relationship, when you are cloistered or imprisoned, a relationship that has the potential to become a long-term friendship, is constructed more easily from timely silences than from ill-timed confessions. Some people even feel so obliged to share autobiographical experiences that they invent them. And it's not always mythomaniacs or liars who do so although there are some of those here as well. Occasionally, they invent an episode out of kindness, as an act of courtesy towards their cellmate, believing it will entertain them, or help them forget their helplessness, or aid them to emerge from a pit of anguish, or revive their nostalgia and rekindle their memory, or even to pass the virus of fictional recollections on to them. Human beings are strange creatures when condemned to their own solitude, or when punishment consists in bringing them face to face every day with the loneliness of one, two or three of their fellows, when none of them ever chose to be in such close proximity. I don't believe (not even after these recent harsh years) what that gloomy existentialist said about hell being other people, but I will admit that often other people are not exactly heaven.

Battered and Bruised
(The sleeping man)

Early evening. Silence outside and inside. If she chooses to look out through the shutters, Graciela knows what she will find. Not only will the path to the building be deserted, but so, too, will everything else: the flowerbeds, the streets within the development, the windows, the narrow balconies of Block B.

The only inhabitants on the move at this time of day are some strange bumblebees that come buzzing up to the shutters, but cannot find a way in. Every so often, from afar, a long way off, as if in almost imperceptible waves, come the sounds of shouting and laughter from a mixed-sex school twelve or fifteen blocks away.

So why bother to get up to look out of the shutters if she already knows what she'll see? In the world outside, everything is routine; but here, inside, in bed, for example, there is something new.

Graciela stubs out her cigarette in an ashtray on the bedside table. She sits up halfway, leaning on her elbow. She studies her own naked body and feels a shiver run through it, but makes no attempt to reach for the sheet that lies crumpled at the foot of the bed.

She is still staring at the shutters, but nothing there rouses her interest. It is probably simply a way of turning her back on the rest of the bed, but she isn't rejecting it; it's more like the postponement of pleasure. Then, before turning round, before looking, she slowly moves her hand until it comes to rest on the sleeping man's skin.

He twitches, like horses do when they are trying to shake off flies. The hand pays no attention to this and stays there stubbornly until the flesh is still again. Then Graciela turns her raised body to completely face the sleeping man. Still covering an archipelago of freckles with her hand, she sweeps her eyes over his body, up and down and back again, pausing at different points, nooks, tiny territories that over the previous few hours she has come to cherish and have sent her compass haywire.

She pauses, for instance, at the heavy shoulder that a few hours earlier she had caressed with her ear and cheek; at the downy chest; the strange, childlike belly button, staring back at her like an astonished eye, as it moves to the rhythm of his breathing; at the deep scar on his hip, the one he got in a barracks which he never mentions; at the unruly reddish hair of the lower triangle; at the magic sex resting now after all that commotion; and at the testicles that are uneven because the left one never recovered, but remains bruised and shrunken after the torture in that same nameless barracks; at the sturdy legs of the 800-metre hurdler he once was; at the rough, big feet, with their long, slightly twisted toes with one nail about to become ingrown.

Graciela removes her hand from this bodily terrain, and brings her mouth close to the other mouth. At that precise moment, a smile appears on the lips of the man, who may still be dreaming, and so she decides to pull back to get a better view of it, to imagine it more clearly, until the smile becomes a sigh or a gasp and then gradually vanishes until it is no more than a half-open mouth once again. She withdraws her own mouth, lips pursed.

Now she is lying on her back, hands behind her head as she stares up at the ceiling. From outside the silence still seeps in, along with the drone of the bumblebees, only now the laughter and shouts from the school can no longer be heard.

This isn't Beatriz's school and it doesn't keep the same hours as hers, but Graciela raises her arm until she can see the time on her digital watch, a gift from her father-in-law. Moving her arm back behind her head, she says softly, as if to avoid waking the sleeping man too brusquely:

'Rolando.'

The sleeping man barely moves. He slowly stretches out a leg and, without opening his eyes, lays his hand on the smooth belly of the wakeful woman.

'Rolando. Up you get. Beatriz will be here in an hour.'

The Other
(Shadows and darkness)

The worst bit was letting time slip by without coming to an agreement about the future. Because it didn't matter how many hours they spent talking about it or how often they plucked up the courage to raise the subject. All the arguments for and against came to nothing when he, Rolando Asuero, repeated once more that now classic gesture, that of the first day of Creation, taking her face in his hands and kissing her with a conviction that each time was more solid and mature, and left a more beguiling trace. And when he took off her clothes just as carefully and pleasurably as the first time, and she let herself be caressed and caressed him in return with a bodily joy that as it lit her up rapidly transformed her from seduced to seducer, that was the end of all the humiliations and pangs of conscience and arbitrary efforts to put themselves in the shoes of the absent one. They never made love at night, because Graciela did not want Beatriz to find out before Santiago himself knew. Graciela did not want her daughter, with a bemused look or by unintentionally overhearing something, to convert what was a clean, transparent act into a covert one, their mutual need into a mystery to be solved. That was why they got together in the afternoons, while the city was taking its siesta and the hum of the bumblebees buzzing round the flowers or at the shutters was the only sound to be heard.

Graciela had confessed that this set schedule had helped her overcome one of her oldest prejudices, more deeply rooted in her habits than she had ever thought she was or had admitted to herself. She had never made love to Santiago in the afternoon, preferring complete darkness – to her, the sense of touch was supreme in any loving union. Santiago, who did not agree about the exclusive pre-eminence of touch, had nevertheless reluctantly resigned himself to her demand, which he attributed to nothing more than a poorly assimilated puritanism, and, above all, to her education at a convent school. There's no going against heaven, he used to say to justify his inevitable concession to her. Graciela, though, had always steadfastly maintained that the Sisters were not to blame, that the ultimate responsibility was hers, because of an obscure sense of shame of which she wasn't proud. Rolando, for his part, pretended to be very liberal and magnanimous, although in reality he was not at all happy with the details she went into of the nights she had spent naked with another man, and simply to exact a petty revenge, had asked her, What about before Santiago then, and she didn't react indignantly, but was slightly ashamed to confess that before Santiago there was no one, and began to go on about the problem of shadows and darkness, saying, You've got the proof now, because making love as we do at siesta-time, even with the shutters closed, the semi-darkness is so luminous that everything is perfectly visible. Her desire for this other body was so strong, so overwhelming, the pleasure of uniting with him so tender, that at no moment had she insisted on her out-of-date need for darkness, and not only had she not abandoned her desire to touch and be touched, but had discovered, almost against her will, to what extent touch was amplified by the decision to look at the other's body in all its manoeuvres, routines and new propositions, and to what extent the sense of touch was amplified when she was being looked at in all her mossy valleys, her hills. Only after the pleasure and release, when he, Rolando Asuero, lit a cigarette and then a second one and passed it to her, only then – or rather a short while later when she returned from the bathroom and cuddled up against him – it was only then that the absent person became present again between them, between the two sated, limp bodies.

She would talk and talk, examining the situation from every angle. She even said that she had never enjoyed her own body as much as she did now, she had never derived so much pleasure, both physically and spiritually, from an act that, after all, did not have that many variations (Rolando does not completely agree with this, but does no more than smile) and yet this sense of fullness did not lead her to make comparisons, because she didn't want to insult the memory of Santiago or even the memory of his body (at this point Rolando stops smiling), she had no wish to tarnish his image in any way, and besides she had no right to do so, because she couldn't forget that when Santiago and she did it, they were younger, more passionate, perhaps more alive (at this point Rolando frowns), but also less experienced, and in addition all their own and other people's suffering in recent years had made them tougher and yet at the same time more tender, made them more real and yet more unreal; as men and women, more definite and, yet also more responsive to their imagination, and all this, all this collapse of rituals and norms, this contradiction between past and present, present and future, all this brand-new objectivity, free from superstition (a smile from Rolando, then a heavy sigh) and melancholy, suddenly became the only rays of light in a sad story: to be less deceitful and less unjust in their dealings with one another, to be better kinds of third-class human beings – because the first- and second-class ones were no longer there, or had perhaps only ever belonged to the realms of fiction and pretence.

Until one afternoon, when they were making love again and

she once more began her post-aphrodisiacal litany, Rolando stubbed out his cigarette, took hers away and put it out as well, gently gripped a loose strand of her hair, laid her down gently and climbed without rushing on top of her astonished, quivering body, and after kissing her close to her ear, said simply: Graciela, don't start all that again, we both know the whole story backwards, so who are you telling it to? He's your husband and I'm his friend, and besides he's a great guy, but we can't go on playing ping-pong with our consciences, can we? We have to choose and it looks as if we have already chosen. We've found something that's very important to us, and so we're going to stick together, despite all the problems and upsets that it implies. The next chapters will be hard, but we're going to stick together. You know it, and I know it. So, let's leave the Santiago question for the day when he's in a fit state to know about it, to adapt to the new reality. You and Don Rafael decided not to say anything to him while he's in prison. I'm not so sure that's the right course of action; don't forget I've been in prison, too and I think I know how people inside view these things, and yet I've accepted your choice, and also my own responsibility within that choice. If, in spite of everything, you still respect Santiago, and so do I, we can't go on talking obsessively about him every time we make love. Obviously, you'll go on thinking about it, and so will I, each of us, on our own account. He paused, kissed her again, and when he, Rolando Asuero, was good and ready, explained it as best he could: the mere fact of not going over and over the matter with words that became worn out and wore them out, that simple silence would be of help to them, would help them love each other as they really were, and not as they felt they had this overly scrupulous obligation to be.

Exiles
(Goodbye and welcome)

Holweide is a district of Cologne, in West Germany. Better call it Köln, so as not to confuse it with the Colonia del Sacramento in Uruguay. It was in Holweide that a Uruguayan family settled (in a temporary fashion that's already lasted seven years). They are Olga and her three children, who in 1974 were only little and now are adolescents. An incomplete family, because their father, David Cámpora, has been in prison in Uruguay since 1971. The school where his three children – Ariel, Silvia and Pablo – are still studying played a decisive role in his release in 1980.

According to the Cámporas: 'Holweide is a working-class district, a slice of German life. There are all sorts: working people and those on the margins of society, sports arenas, small businesses, kindly old ladies and gossipy old ladies, several churches, a couple of banks, a pilot school that is very progressive: in other words, ordinary people.'

'The school was opened,' Olga tells me, 'just when my kids started to attend. It now has twelve hundred pupils. Everyone took part in the efforts made to secure David's release: parents, teachers, pupils, the headmistress and even the Ministry of Education, which recognized that for this school human rights were more than just a theory class. A Cámpora committee was set up. We met once a fortnight to brainstorm what new efforts we could make. Sometimes we thought there was nothing more we could do; but then a new idea always arose.'

Several meetings for Uruguay were held. For the first, the school called together parents to inform them about David's situation and to consult them about what could be done. 'We were expecting around thirty people to come,' says Olga, 'but to our surprise, some five hundred turned up. At the meeting, it was decided to hold a demonstration outside the Uruguayan Embassy. Buses were hired, funds collected; we even had to pay insurance for the children, because holding the demonstration meant taking them from Köln to Bonn. Some children contributed by giving us part of their monthly allowance. The total cost was 4,000 marks, and more than 800 people took part. That's a lot here, especially considering the youngest children had to be accompanied by their parents or bring written permission. That was the start of a busy series of activities. Twenty thousand letters, and as many signatures, were sent to the Uruguayan government. Thirteen schools in the city joined in. Articles were published in the press, and the Cámpora case became widely known and taken up as a personal matter. Respectable housewives, who had never handed out leaflets before, began to collect signatures and explain what was going on in Uruguay. A few people said, "If he's in jail, there must be a reason," but they were pretty much the exception.'

That supportive community lived with all the family's own ups and downs, their hopes of release, and their disappointments at the abrupt refusals made by the dictatorship. 'At last, and before David did himself, we learned that his freedom was imminent, and the headmistress asked us what we could do for his arrival, to welcome him, because so many parents wanted to go and greet him at the airport. It was clear to us that those who had done so much to secure his freedom had every right to share our joy. I went ahead to Frankfurt to warn David, because, for obvious reasons, he was unaware of all that had been done on his behalf. Then, at Köln Airport, three hundred people were waiting for him; children with drawings, and flowers, and apples, as gifts. There were many tears as well.

'It was decided that a big party would be held at the school, so that everyone could see and touch David; he was their achievement, *their conquest, the result of all of their efforts made in solidarity. Of course, first of all we had to bring him up to speed.'*

There were speeches at the party. Doctor Focke spoke. Aged sixty-five, she was one of the old guard of the Social Democrats; to some extent, she is David's moral guarantor in Germany. 'In fact,' says Olga, 'she is our fairy godmother.' Other speeches came from the school's headmistress, then from a representative of the parents (a construction worker who is one of our best friends here), a pupil ('who has become a brilliant politician'), and a teacher's spokes-woman. Then David had a brief five minutes to express his thanks, although, including the translation (by his daughter Silvia), he took eight. And, finally, a member of parliament spoke, the city mayor and (since different groups working for Latin America had also been invited) a woman representing the FDR from El Salvador. 'And then the dancing started, with music by an orchestra made up of Italian workmen. So there was a great knees-up, with food, drink, tears and all the rest.'

These are the words spoken by David Cámpora on that evening of 20th March 1981: 'Tonight has a special meaning. In some delightful and strange way, we have come to say goodbye, and also to welcome one another. We are saying goodbye, without sadness, to a man who was in prison for nine years. Who was a prisoner because he refused to fold his arms when the people of his country were experiencing hunger, pain and injustice. We are saying goodbye, without forget-ting, to a harsh, drawn-out, but tremendously valuable experience. Every political prisoner ought to thank his jailers for confirming, in his deeds and in his person, the validity of his convictions, of his actions. A man is never surer of what he is doing than when he remains undiscouraged, undefeated, after prolonged suffering. We are saying goodbye to a situation, but our memory of it will remain. And we are also welcoming a father to this school. Three children and a wife have led me here by the hand; they want to show me the excel-lence that nests within human beings. Men and women of the people,* who are capable of giving, and giving of themselves. It is an emotional father, who already feels at home here, who today can say "Hello" to you and ask where we are heading together. I feel within me that this celebration is something special, quite unlike anything else; it is new and important. So incredibly important I cannot find the exact words I need to describe it. So incredibly new, as such warmth always is, the warmth of people who have chosen to love others. There is also greatness here tonight. There is the great imperative to carry on doing, to carry on being able to. An imperative that springs from what has already been achieved. Because you were able to. You were able to overcome the brutality of a dictatorship, the jailers' insistent hatred, the laziness and comfort of life lived only for oneself. You were able to do that, and I am here as a proof of your power. As proof, but not the measure. Because there is no limit to what's possible for those who have learned they can succeed. I dare to speak on behalf of all my many imprisoned brothers, to represent them fully, and to say to you: many thanks for not abandoning us, many thanks for loving us so much. To ask you to persist in your solidarity with Latin America, a continent that is buying the right to be free with its own blood. Tonight, we can talk of prison and death without compromising our joy. Because the joy is that of militant victory, because this party is a celebration of the effort we devoted to the cause. We are happy because we are able to feel the pain of our fellow men. There is no adequate way to thank you for what you have given me. To you I owe the free air, and light, streets and voices, dreams and books. You have given me back my children and my wife: my place of affection, my tenderness. I feel ashamed to be talking to you, saying things. All I want to transmit to you is my faith in mankind and the opaque wisdom of the prisoner. Precisely to you, good, determined people, who have just achieved the impossible. You who know and who can. Tonight is for you, it is you we are honouring. And I am the one who applauds and embraces you.'

The Germans wept; the Latin Americans – well, you can imagine.

With good reason. According to Olga (because David is very discreet) 'a girl kissed him and stroked his back for a long while, thanking him for all he had given her'. In the end, the girl was right. Without knowing or intending to, David had given that community the rare opportunity to realize the best of itself.

Don Rafael
(A country called Lydia)

Am I a foreigner? There are days when I'm sure I am; others
when I don't attach any importance to that at all, and others
still when I in no way admit my foreignness to myself. Can it
be that the condition of being foreign is a state of mind? Probably if I was in Finland or the Cape Verde islands or the Vatican
or in Dallas I'd feel inescapably foreign, but even then, who
knows? And on that note, why do we always start any list of
far-off countries, of distances, of foreign affairs, with Finland?
Who can have put that prejudice into our noggins? For us,
speaking of someone who is in Finland has always been the
equivalent of saying they're in the depths of hell. And if we
don't always associate the two, it's because we've never seen
depths of hell with so much ice and snow. After all, what do we
know of the Finns or the Finlanders, apart from the *Kalevala*
and the Nobel Prize for Sillampää, the one with those four little dots on its two 'a's? Up until the 1952 Olympics, newspapers
in the far south used to write its capital city as 'Helsinski', with
an 's' before the 'k', and then shortly afterwards they started
writing 'Helsinki'. What can have happened during the Olym-
pic Games for Helsinki to lose its second 's'?

But I'm not in Finland. I'm here. And here, am I a foreigner?
Not long ago I read in a good book by a German author about
these ambivalent times: 'It's curious that foreigners first learn
insults, bad language and the current slang of the country they

are living in (a girl who has only lived for a few months in P. already gives cries of pain in French. She says "Aïe!" instead of "Ow!")' According to this definition, I'm not a foreigner because I carry on cursing exactly as I used to in my own 'purple' land. And when I'm feeling intense pain I don't shout out any interjection, imported or home-grown, I merely let out a strange sound that could be defined as onomatopoeic, even though the dictionary offers only three examples of onomatopoeia (meow, glug-glug, ker-pow!) that of course, fortunately, have nothing to do with the grunts or snorts or growls I usually produce on such painful occasions.

What would I have thought of myself last month, for instance, on Wednesday the 9th to be exact, if I had shouted glug-glug or ker-pow! when Professor Ordóñez trapped my finger in the very solid door of his Volkswagen? Instead, my modest, guttural groan, together with a withering look ('withering' not in the sense of 'dying' but 'cutting'), must have left poor Ordóñez without the slightest doubt as to my instantaneous hatred of him – a hatred as unjust as it was instantaneous, because he had squashed my first finger only due to a moment of unforgivable distraction and not out of any aggressive xenophobia. I must confess, however, that at the time the certainty that this idiot would be capable, with as much equanimity and equal clumsiness, of butchering the finger of any of his *own* beloved countrymen did little to make me feel better. It might sound like a lie, but that unfortunate incident seemed fortunate to me, because for a good few minutes we must have been like two 'pale faces' together (luckily no Sioux appeared on the horizon): me, because I was about to pass out in the middle of one of my guttural groans, and Ordóñez for much the same reason: the only difference being that it was *my* finger which was injured. Now, would I have felt the same degree of instantaneous hatred (which I admit was unjust) towards my colleague even when I was on the point of passing out, if the owner of the Volkswagen had been a Uruguayan from Paso Molino, Tambores or Palmitas? I have my doubts, but since the only way to resolve them would be for a compatriot from Paso Molino, Tambores or Palmitas to crush my finger in the door of his Volkswagen (bah, it could be another model), I'm more than happy to remain in the precarious but decidedly more comfortable territory of philosophical doubt. And anyway, even if my instantaneous hatred of the tiresome Ordóñez had international connotations, or, at least, inter-Latin American ones, my case would not be one of xenophobia, but quite the opposite.

A forced transplantation is difficult at any age. I've experienced that for myself. But possibly it's young people who feel most punished. And I'm not saying this because of Graciela, or Rolando, or even for Santiago, when, eventually, he's set free. I'm thinking more of the youngsters who were still little kids when all the trouble kicked off. It must be almost impossible for them to see this stage in their lives as something that *isn't* transitory, but a long-term frustration. And the danger is that this feeling could turn them into the victims of an irreversible erosion.

How many of those we saw being such gutsy militants in La Teja or Malvín or Industrias and now see in Paris near the Sacré-Coeur, or the Ponte Vecchio in Florence, or Madrid's Rastro, stretched out beside handicrafts they themselves have made or woven, how many of those young men and women with their vague smiles and distant gazes, have not seen, months or years earlier, how their most beloved comrades fell? Or have heard terrifying shouts from the stinking next-door cell? How can one fairly judge these neo-pessimists, these premature sceptics, if we don't start by understanding that their hopes have been abruptly mutilated? How can we forget that these young people, separated from their surround-ings, families, friends, their classrooms, have been denied their basic human right, to rebel as youngsters, to fight as youngsters? The only right they've been left with is to die as youngsters.

Sometimes these young people demonstrate bullet-proof courage, and yet their minds are not disappointment-proof. If only I and other veterans could convince them that their duty is to stay young. Not to grow old out of nostalgia, boredom or rancour, but to stay young, so that when the time comes to go back they do so as young people and not as the relics of past rebelliousness. As youngsters – that is – as life.

After that outburst I think I've earned the right to a deep breath. There's no doubt that when I am serious I'm unbear-able. But it may also be that this is the real Rafael Aguirre: the unbearable, annoying, rhetorical one, and that the other Rafael Aguirre, the one who enjoys making plays on words, who mocks others a little and himself a lot, is in reality a mask for this one.

Perhaps that's a roundabout way of replying to my own question: am I a foreigner? And I answer myself this way, with one hand, the right one, in the shroud, and the other, the left, drawing a sun that I wish was as spontaneous and luminous as the one my granddaughter draws, with her startling and inso-lent colours. Except that I can't draw a green sun and pink clouds like she does, without the slightest sky rhetoric. In the end, I think that in me the sun is more powerful (even though it is an orthodox yellow and orange) than the shroud.

The only thing that can redeem an old man is, however hard it may be, for him to feel young. Mind you, I said young, and not stupid. Not for him to pretend to be a kid wearing brash colours or listening to that crap that blasts out in discotheques (oh, the incomparable Beatles of my pre-old age, with their

'Michelle', or 'Yesterday', or 'Eleanor Rigby'), but to feel, with great and seasoned difficulty, that he is an old young man.

Possibly that was the first thing Lydia understood, and possibly that (I mean the fact that she understood it) was the first thing I liked about her. And without too many illusions. Perhaps it happened like that because she is from here, because she is not my compatriot. No one can or wants to be free of their nostalgias, but exile shouldn't become frustration. To create links with and work with the people of this country, as if they were our own people, is the best way for us to feel useful, and there's no better antidote to frustration than to feel useful.

To create links with the people from this country. Well, I have links to Lydia. As I sometimes tell her: after all, as you can see, I am learning with Lydia. And I feel better. The pretence of the walking stick is a long way behind me. This is also why I don't feel foreign, because she isn't my *foreigner*, but something like *my woman*. She has her percentage of indigenous blood, thank goodness. Or perhaps it's her black heritage, thank goodness again. Let's just say that her lovely skin is darker than that of Graciela or Beatriz. And even darker (and much less wrinkled) than mine.

Perhaps I have links with a country called Lydia. And a bond that's different from all my previous ones. Several classic ingredients are missing: urgency, passion, that tight feeling in the chest. I wouldn't go so far as to say I'm in love, but maybe I dare think it. Obviously, if I make the mistake of looking at myself in the mirror, I come to my senses. There is no (nor is there likely to be) marriage, but what I can't deny is that, if Lydia isn't from my own village, she is from my caste, my tribe. And when I say I have links to the country of Lydia, it's not just a figure of speech; because she was the one who introduced me to things, the meals, the people from here. I've already begun to celebrate (though not to use, of course) the local idioms, and not only the established ones, but personal ones as well, such as, for example, when Lydia's sister-in-law's husband says he feels like twitching his moustache, that means he's hoping to have lunch.

Despite this, I still see my compatriots. There are loads of topics I can talk about only with them, I mean talk openly, aware of the context, although not always so aware of the consequences. To weigh up the complicated balance of the past, especially their more difficult recent one, or as my good friend Valdés says (general medicine and respiratory tracts) with his professional quirkiness: 'We need to take a stethoscope to the country, gentlemen, put our ear to its back and then tell it: say thirty-three, please, say Thirty-Three Orientales.'*

But by now, that's not enough. I can't live here that way, with the obsession that tomorrow or next October or in two years I'm going to slip my moorings and embark on my return, the mythical return, because living provisionally like that is always incomplete, so when I explore inside the country of Lydia, and that's much more than a sexual allusion (although admittedly I do explore inside there and it's a great trip), it's also to discover what the inhabitants of country Lydia are discovering, it's listening to the news on radio and TV from start to finish, and not only when it's about international affairs, in the daily anticipation that at last something good will arrive from down there. But what does arrive is that another four people have disappeared, or three died in prison and not always because of what a certain defenestrated president used to call 'the rigour and demands of interrogation', but purely and simply out of weariness and being over-saturated with prison.

---

* Treinta y Tres Orientales: These were the thirty-three leaders of the revolt in 1825 which led to the liberation of the Oriental Province from Brazil and the establishment of Uruguay as an independent nation.

What arrives is that there were more 'sweeps', and five hundred people were arrested, then as expected they released four hundred and twenty, but who were the other eighty, and what will they do to them?

We're losing the healthy habit of hope. We find it almost impossible to comprehend that other societies do generate it. I remember the early hours of the 30th of November. I had told Lydia not to come. I wanted to be alone with my scepticism. I didn't believe in the plebiscite; it seemed to me a ridiculous trap. But I woke up at three in the morning and had a feeling I should turn on the short-wave radio. And the news came mingled with my dream (which hadn't been particularly encouraging) and the 'No' vote had demolished the military's proposal. And it was only once I had convinced myself this wasn't some postscript to my dream that I jumped out of bed and shouted as if I was in the football stadium and suddenly I realized I was crying (without any sense of shame) and was even sobbing and that those tears weren't corny or ridiculous. I was so surprised at my own outburst that I tried to remember the last time I had cried like that. I had to go back to October 1967, in Montevideo, when I was also alone in the night, when another short-wave radio station had detailed the sad news given by Fidel about Che's death.

But in November 1980 the people of Country Lydia let me weep alone, and I thanked them for it. They only came round the next day, to hug me after checking that my eyes were dry, so that I could explain the inexplicable to them. And so I told them while at the same time I was convincing myself: the dictatorship had decided to open, not a door, but a crack, one that was so small that only a single syllable could enter, and so the people saw that crack and without giving it a second thought slipped the syllable 'No' inside it. It's probable that tomorrow the military will slam the door and again close the fortress they believed was impregnable, but by then, it will be too late, it will be impossible for them to get rid of it. In this era of neutron bombs and nuclear warheads, it's amazing the power that one poor negative syllable can have.

And Lydia came round, of course (not the country of Lydia, but Lydia herself and her soul). She didn't say a word, and I was grateful to her for that, and after also making sure I was dry-eyed, she sat on the floor next to me (as usual I was in the rocking-chair, and I stopped rocking) and laid her dark head and black hair in my lap.

Beatriz
(Amnesty)

'Amnesty' is a difficult word, or as Grandpa Rafael says, very challenging. That's because it has an 'm' and an 'n' that always go together. Amnesty is when someone has a punishment pardoned. For example, if I come home from school in dirty clothes and Graciela, that is my mum, tells me, You won't have any puddings for a week, and if then afterwards I behave and three days later I bring home good marks in arithmetic, she gives me an amnesty and I can eat those ice creams they call 'boats' again. They have three scoops, one vanilla, another chocolate and a third that's strawberry, though Grandpa Rafael calls that fruit something different, like in Uruguay.

Also when Teresita and I had really fallen out because she gave me a muddy slap and we spent like, two weeks without even saying goodbye to each other or lending each other our toothbrushes, then suddenly I saw that the poor thing was very sorry and couldn't live without my affection and I realized she sighed whenever I went past her and I grew scared she could commit suicide like on the TV, so I called her and told her, Look, Teresita, I amnesty you, but she thought I had called her only to insult her and burst into tears so badly I had to say – Teresita, don't be such a donkey, 'I amnesty you' means 'I pardon you', and that set her off crying again, but this time it was different, it was out of emotion.

Also the other day on TV I saw a bullfight, which is like a

stadium where a man plays with a red blanket and a bull who pretends to be furious, but is really very good, and after playing like this for many, many hours the man grew bored and said, I don't want to play any more with this animal that's pretending to be furious, but the bull wanted to go on playing, so then it was the man who grew furious, and because he was very silly he stuck a very long sword here, in the back of its head, and the bull, who was about to ask the man for amnesty, looked at him with such very sad eyes and then fainted in the middle of the pitch without anybody giving him amnesty and that made me so upset I gave a low sigh and that night, I dreamt I was stroking the bull and saying to him, Here, boy, here, boy, just like I say to Irony, Angélica's dog, and he wags his tail with delight, but in the dream the bull didn't wag his, because he was still lying there in the middle of the pitch, and I gave him an amnesty, but it doesn't work in dreams.

The dictionary says that amnesty means to forget political offences, so I was thinking that maybe they'll give Dad an amnesty, but I'm also afraid that the general who made him a political prisoner has a good memory and doesn't forget offences. Of course, seeing that my dad is so very, very good and even knows how to sweep out the cells, maybe the general who made him a political prisoner will overlook it, just like my grandpa does with me, as if he has forgotten the offences even if he hasn't really forgotten them, and maybe one night the general who made my dad a political prisoner will give him amnesty all of a sudden and, without telling him, leave the door unlocked so that my dad can tiptoe out and go quietly into the street and find a taxi and tell the driver, really pleased, that he has just been given an amnesty and so he should take him straightaway to the airport because he wants to come and see Graciela and me, and he'll say to the driver, I've got a little girl I haven't seen for many years, but who I know is very pretty and very good, and the driver will say, How interesting, I also have a little girl, and they'll go on talking and talking because the airport is a huge amount of kilometres away, so that by the time they arrive it'll already be night-time, and my dad will say, The problem is that because I was a political prisoner I don't have any money to pay you, and the driver, Don't you worry, friend, it's only thirty-eight million, you pay me when you can and have got a job, and my dad, You're very kind many thanks, and the driver, Think nothing of it and give your wife my best wishes and your daughter who is so good and so pretty, and, have a good trip and congratulations on the amnesty.

Angélica, though, is very vindictive, and when Irony bites her only a little because he has tiny teeth and doesn't mean it, she hits him and beats him and doesn't speak to him for three days, and I know Irony is dying of sadness and yet she never amnesties him. I feel very sorry for little Irony and I'd love to take him home, but Graciela always says that in exile you shouldn't have pets because you'd only grow fond of them and then all of a sudden you have to go back to Montevideo and we can't take the dog or cat because they would wee in the plane.

When the amnesty comes we're going to dance tangos. Tangos are sad music that you dance to when you're happy so that you'll feel sad again. When the amnesty comes Graciela is going to buy me a new doll because Monica is ready for the scrapheap. When the amnesty comes there'll be no more bullfights and I won't have any more spots. And Grandpa Rafael is going to buy me a wristwatch. When the amnesty comes there'll be no more amnesia. Amnesty is like a holiday that's going to spread through the whole country. Planes and boats will arrive packed with tourists loaded with money who will come to see the amnesty. The planes will be so full that people will be standing in the aisles and the ladies will say to the gentlemen who have got seats, Ah so you're going to see the amnesty as well, and then the gentleman will have to give her his seat. When the amnesty comes, there'll be spoons and T-shirts and ashtrays with the word amnesty on them and also dolls that when you press their belly-buttons will say 'Am-*nes*-ty' and play a little tune. When the amnesty comes it will mean no more times tables, especially those of eight and nine, that are rubbish. I imagine that when my dad comes someday, he's going to talk for like a year about the amnesty. Teresita says that Sandra said that in very cold countries there is less amnesty, but I think it can't be as bad there, because since it's snowing outside and an icy wind is blowing, the political prisoners won't want to be set free because they're snug and warm in their cells. I sometimes think the amnesty is taking so long that maybe by the time it comes I'll be as old as Graciela and I'll work in a skyscraper and I'll even be able to cross streets on a red light like grown-ups always do. When the amnesty comes, maybe Graciela will say to Rolando, OK, *ciao*.

The Other
(Put on your body)

So, you find me strange? That's possible, Rolando, it's possible. Besides, we haven't seen each other in a long while. And yet I ought to be happy. And maybe I am happy and that's what makes me seem strange. Do you think that's impossible? We're so accustomed to deaths, that when, by contrast, there's a birth it catches us unawares, or as a local baseball fan would say (you can see how I'm adapting) it 'catches us off base'. You must be asking yourself what has happened. And you find it hard to accept this might be something encouraging. You're suspicious of it, aren't you? I've become suspicious, too. And yet this new factor is good news: they've released Claudia and she's in Sweden. That wasn't what you imagined, was it? Well, they released her and she is in Sweden; she's already written to me and I've written back. What do you make of that? Six years is a very long time, especially considering I could escape (only just, but I made it), whereas she didn't: she had to swallow those six years of shit, humiliations, of rotting, of craziness. Now tell me: how could I enjoy my own freedom, or my job (at last I'm doing something I like, something that corresponds to my training), or the simple fact of being able to say out loud whatever I wanted to, how was I going to enjoy life when I knew Claudia was back there, crushed, courageous but badly hurt, loyal but filled with anxiety? I'm thirty-two years old; I'm strong and sexually healthy, full of vitality. You know that if you're normal, at my age, it's impossible to go six years without occasionally having sex with a woman. I know that as well, and so does Claudia. In her letters she has suggested it in a roundabout way, and by other channels she told me so straight out: 'Don't make it a problem, Angel. I love you more than ever, but I can't demand that of you. You're a young man and you're outside. You can't deny what your body wants. It's *your* body. I'm not going to feel offended. Ever. I'm being serious. Please believe me. Later on, when I get out, we'll see what happens. Yes, I still love you more than ever, but don't be without a woman, don't condemn yourself to live without the body of a woman. I, more than anyone, know how much you need it.' The same message, over and over. All that was lacking was for her to write that verse of Vallejo's: 'The day will come. Put on your body.' It was almost an obsession in her letters and messages. I always answered that she wasn't to worry, that it was a possibility, later on, but that for now I had no wish or desire for anything like that. But she kept on insisting. Until finally a situation arose which I had not been looking for, something that happened very naturally, and I decided to put on my body. I mean, I went to bed with a tremendous girl, and obviously we did it, but, on another level, it was a failure. I watched myself jigging about as if it were someone else. Of course, my organs reacted when they came into close contact with a beautiful body: they performed, were aroused, reached a climax all on their own, but I remained distant from the pleasure. There I was, in a remote cell, whispering support for a distant woman who was mine, not touching her but trying to console her for wounds that will never heal, whispering words, little disjointed words that for the two of us make up our secret ritual, like landmarks in our private history. You'll say this happens with every couple. Ah, but in this couple, one was here, free but feeling stupidly guilty about his freedom, and the other one was over there, imprisoned but still fighting, accompanied, but all alone, probably thinking of me and how I was feeling stupidly guilty about my freedom. And the girl who was in bed with me suddenly understood the situation quite clearly, and did so despite being from here, or perhaps because of that, and when we were lying on our backs staring up at the ceiling in silence, she rested her hand on my leg and said: 'Don't worry, it's because you're a good person.' With that she got up, kissed me on the cheek, and left. So just think what good news it was for me to know that after six years, the other woman, the only woman, the punished, loyal one, was free and in Sweden with friends. That's the story. So far. We've written to one another, phoned. And let me tell you that the phone is not an ideal means of communication, because we were both in floods of tears, and it ended up costing us a pile of money just to spend a quarter of an hour listening to three monosyllables and four sobs. From the first I wrote that she should come at once. I even bought her an open plane ticket so that she could travel whenever she wanted and was able to. But in her reply, I noted a certain reticence, and I began to imagine absurd things. Just imagine the freedom you must have when you start imagining absurd things. Reasonable ones have to do with permits, residencies, passports and so on, but I chose the others, or some of them at least, and listed them for her in my latest letter. And today I received her reply. I'll read it to you: 'You're still thinking of the Claudia you last saw six years ago, but many things have happened during those six years and even faces change. That transformation occurs at a different rate to the simple passage of time. I know that you, for example, look the same, only six years older. That's normal, isn't it? But as for me, my love, I don't have the same face. That's the reticence you noticed in my letter. And since you imagined such crazy stuff, I came to this decision: I took several photos of myself, and although you won't believe it, I chose the best. I'm sending it to you now. And, Angel, before you decide whether I should go there or stay here, I want you to see how I am and how I look. You'll see how those six years have passed for my eyes, mouth, nose, ears, forehead, hair. And if you truly love and respect me (you know I'm a Catholic, so I'm asking you this for the love of God), I want you to be strictly honest with me.' Rolando, do you realize what she's saying in that letter? Can you read everything between the lines like I can? That's why I said before that maybe I'm happy, and that's what makes me somewhat strange. I feel happy, and yet I'm not happy. I never imagined that to feel happy would contain so much sadness.

Battered and Bruised
(Life's a bitch)

'And what did you feel when he read you the letter, and told you about the photo?'

'Bewildered. Really, I think I felt bewildered.'

'Bewildered and guilty?'

'No, not guilty.'

'So why did you come here with a face like a funeral?'

'Maybe because this mess isn't exactly a fiesta.'

'When you say "mess", do you mean us?'

'Yes, what else?'

'I don't see it as a mess.'

'You don't? Well, it is.'

'Are you sorry about it?'

'No, but it's no fiesta.'

'You already said that. Their situation is no fiesta either.'

'Claudia and Angel's situation? No, it isn't. But at least it's transparent. A transparent pain. A transparent love.'

'Unlike ours, which is opaque.'

'I didn't say that.'

'But that's what you're implying. Everything you don't say openly, you're still saying. You think I don't tell myself that as well?'

'You know that, for me, the only thing that's opaque is that we haven't told Santiago. Nothing else. I really love you, Graciela, and that's not opaque.'

'Why go over that again? I talked to Rafael about it and he convinced me not to. And I still think he was right. It was too much for Santiago. To learn that way, and to learn while he was in there. Shut inside four walls.'

'Well, now he's getting out.'

'Yes, and I'm pleased he is.'

'Pleased he's coming means you're sorry about the rest?'

'No, Rolando, I'm not sorry either. "Pleased" means "pleased", nothing more. Pleased because he'll be free, and he deserves it. And also, because I'll be able to tell him.'

'You'll be able to?'

'Yes, Rolando, I will. I'm quite a lot stronger than you think. And besides, I'm sure of it. I'm convinced that the other way would be a mistake. And I respect Santiago too much to go on lying to him.'

'Life's a bitch, isn't it? For a guy to get out after so many years, and find this waiting for him. I mean: to find us waiting for him with this great piece of news.'

'I don't know. After all, as Rafael says, it's better for him to find out here, with a different perspective.'

'The others will find out as well. His comrades. Did your beloved Rafael mention that?'

'No, but I'm well aware of it.'

'I don't think they're going to be on our side.'

'Probably not. Everyone loves Santiago. It'll be difficult.'

'How are you going to tell him?'

'I don't know, Rolando, I don't know.'

'Would you prefer the two of us to talk to him together?'

'Look, I don't know how I'm going to tell him. I'll think of something. But I do know that I want to tell him on my own. I have that right, don't I?'

'You've every right. What about little Beatriz?'

'She seems distant. And that upsets me as well.'

'Does she know her father is arriving in a fortnight?'

'She's known since last Sunday. I decided to tell her, despite Santiago's warning. Do you know why? Because I thought she had found out or sensed it in some strange way, and that maybe she was being distant because I hadn't told her myself. But she's been just the same since I did tell her.'

'That little kid is too sharp. I'm sure she's suspicious about us.'

'Yes, I think so, too.'

'Well, after all, it's an inevitable reaction.'

'Possibly, but it worries me.'

'So why are you crying now?'

'Because you're right.'

'Of course, but about what?'

'About what you said just now: life's a bitch.'

Exiles
(The proud people of Alamar)

I lived more than two years in Alamar, a place some 15 kilometres from Havana, that consists mostly of blocks of flats in constant construction by brigades of building workers from the capital. That is one of the ways the Cubans have found to try to resolve their chronic housing problem without it affecting production. In every factory, office or warehouse they enlist thirty-three of their employees into construction-work brigades. Since, generally, these are not builders, they begin with a basic course. After that, they start to build buildings of between five and twelve storeys, which are then occupied by those of their colleagues (or sometimes by they themselves) who are in the most urgent need of new housing. The labour shortage each brigade leaves in its original workplace is made up by the others there working overtime. Curiously, the idea came from the workers themselves; the government simply put it into practice.

But there is another detail which concerns us directly. In each of these new buildings the construction-work brigades keep one flat (if it is a five-storey block) or four (if it is twelve storeys high) reserved for families of Latin American exiles, who are welcomed with furniture, a fridge, radio and TV, a gas cooker, and even sheets and crockery. All for free.

This means that a fair number of Latin Americans are concentrated in Alamar. The Uruguayan children and adolescents there are usually, if not bilingual, then at least bi-tonal. When they play and run around the streets with their local friends they speak with a strong Cuban accent. But when they're back home, where their parents still stubbornly and deliberately use Uruguayan expressions like 'vos' and 'che', then they're from the far south of Latin America once again.

Alamar is a pretty spot, maybe with fewer buses and trees than are needed, but the air is gentle and has a salty tang because the sea is close at hand, and there is a sense of undemonstrative solidarity.

On the 30th of November 1980, the day of the plebiscite in Uruguay, when the dictatorship tripped itself up, I wasn't in Alamar, but in Spain. In the early hours of that morning, as the news of the explosive popular triumph spread to the front pages of the world's media, I of course thought many things, but amongst others, I thought of Alamar. It would have been so good to be there to celebrate that incredible victory.

When I visited Havana the following January it was the first topic I brought up with Alfredo Gravina. Alfredo and I have lots of things in common, but above all two very important ones: literature and Tacuarembó, even though he comes from the capital of the department and I'm only from Paso de los Toros.

'Oh, that night.' He rolled up his eyes. I always thought that, with his inimitable sense of calm, Alfredo (whose second name is Dante, but I never dared poke fun at him over that, because my third name is Hamlet) came out of a Vittorio de Sica film, with a screenplay by Cesare Zavattini. Oh, but when he rolls his eyes up he's the spitting image of Totó.

'You know, that night several of us from the Uruguayan colony had got together to chat and have a few drinks. The result of the plebiscite? We were sure it would be a fraud.' A beaming smile appeared among a mass of wrinkles, and spread in a way that those who didn't know him might have thought was mocking, but which, we friends knew, was him laughing at himself. By that, I don't mean self-criticism. There's a subtle difference, isn't there?

'We began singing tangos, old tangos, perhaps as a way of calming *our rosy-hued nostalgia. But one of the women, more of a realist (as women tend to be), had her ear glued to the international radio news. So that was the scene: we were singing Gardel songs and she was listening to the BBC. All of a sudden, she jumped up: "The 'No's won! 'No' won by more than sixty per cent!" Instantly, we all abandoned poor old Gardel and listened to the BBC, which confirmed the astounding news.'*

On that same 30th of November, in Mallorca, I also heard the news on the BBC. Never before had the precise, sterilized Spanish they use, that kind of amalgam between Guadalajara and Ushuaia, seemed so splendid.

'We went out into the street with a flag,' Alfredo continued. 'I've no idea where we found it. We had to tell everyone and celebrate. We knocked on the doors of our compatriots, but most of them had not hesitated, like we had, between Gardel and the BBC. They had simply gone to bed, because Monday is a work day. A lot of them thought it was a joke at first, but gradually we convinced them, and they joined our group, which became more and more enthusiastic and raucous. We made so much noise that the police had no choice but to turn up, slightly amazed at such an uproar in an Alamar which, at that time of night, is only either resting or making love. What was this? What was going on? The clincher was the Uruguayan flag; from then on, they understood everything. They simply suggested we shouldn't make so much noise, but I think they had little expectation we would take their advice. In fact, the celebration only ended when the sun came up.'

So, in the end, how did they feel? 'Proud, che, proud,' said old Alfredo, skinny, wrinkled but standing tall, his chest puffed out as if he was back in Tacuarembó.

Don Rafael
(Clearing the rubble)

It's odd. My son is about to leave prison, he's going to arrive here someday soon, and I receive the news completely naturally, almost as if it were the corollary of a premonition. Was it really so foreseeable? How many, even with fewer years inside than Santiago, found one day that they could no longer bear their anguish, their cancer, their own story, and died? And yet right from the start I knew he would get out. Possibly by instinct, a father's sixth sense. What's even odder is that when Graciela told me, at that first revelatory moment, it wasn't him or me or my granddaughter or the big problem awaiting him here that I thought of. I thought only of his mother, Mercedes. I thought of her as if she were still alive, as if my legitimate, reasonable impulse was to go and run to tell her, inform her that soon she would be able to embrace him, hug him, stroke his cheeks, cry on his shoulder, who knows what. This was when I realized that, despite all the years that have passed, despite Lydia today and other women yesterday and before that, there is still a private link between me and Mercedes, to the name and memory of Mercedes, always dressed in brown; her tranquil gaze, which, deep down, always held a hint of emotion; her weak, yet safe, hands; her unmistakable, often hermetic smile; her tender concern for Santiago. Sometimes it seems to me (and it's no more crazy than anything else), that she would have liked to have a screen behind which she could talk to Santiago, caress Santiago, look at Santiago, without the rest of the world (me among them) bothering her with their curiosity, deference or suspicion. But since, of course, there was no such screen, she suffered rather, although without any fuss, in moderation, as was her style. Mercedes was not ugly. Nor pretty. She had a face that was one of a kind: attractive, impossible to confuse or forget. And a kindness that was complex but real. Now, at this great distance, if I wished to be absolutely frank with myself, maybe I wouldn't be able to recognize what I fell in love with, or if I ever really fell in love with that excessively private woman. That's what I tell myself, and then immediately sense I'm being unfair. It's obvious I must have fallen in love. It's just that I don't remember it. We used to talk to each other less than an ordinary couple does, but then again, we weren't an ordinary couple. And those few conversations we had were definitely not ordinary. She often flummoxed me, but I could never offend her, shout at her, or blame her for anything. She always seemed like a survivor from a shipwreck who had still not entirely come to terms with her survival. I found it hard to communicate with her, but on the few occasions I did, it was a miraculous, almost magical communication. Perhaps making love to Mercedes was like making love to a concept, rather than a body, but afterwards she was so sweet and tremulous that this epilogue meant a much closer union than the act itself. It was only when she listened to good music that she regained the expression of a model for a Filippo Lippi fresco. After no more than two years of married life, in one of her rare bursts of confidence that were like concessions she made to us (to herself and to me) she said how good it would be to die listening to one of Vivaldi's *Four Seasons*. And all those years later, on exactly the 17th of June, 1958, when she was reading and all of a sudden remained still for ever, on the radio (not even on the record-player) they were playing 'Spring'. Santiago heard this, and maybe that's why that word, 'spring', has always been so linked to his life. It's like his thermometer, his reference point, his norm. Even though he has only mentioned it on very rare occasions, I know that for him events in the world in general and in his own world in particular are divided into spring-like, not very spring-like, and definitely un-spring-like. I imagine these last five years won't have seemed very spring-like to him. And now he's coming out. Was it wrong of me to advise Graciela not to write to him about the new reality? There are only twelve days to go before I find out. Or maybe six months or six years will have to go by for me properly to learn whether my advice was correct or if I goofed. Life goes on, as banal songs never tire of telling us, or if they don't say that, they suggest it. And just because they're banal songs, we brainy types completely reject their schmaltz. And yet there's always a nugget of truth in everything schmaltzy. Life goes on, of course it does, but there's not only one way for it to do so. Everybody has their own route and destination. I know (because Graciela herself told me the story) about the clear-cut case of that couple Angel and Claudia (I think he was one of my students). For them, life went on in the same tender, moving way. But there's no guarantee. In fact, their story is moving and tender precisely because it happened without any inner violence, with an absolutely natural inevitability. I trust Santiago. I think that however much he loved and admired his mother, deep down, he has more of me in him than of her. So, I imagine what I would do, what my attitude would be in a case like his. And that's why I trust Santiago. It's obvious that I'm sixty-seven and he's only thirty-eight. But there's little Beatriz, who is so wonderful and who, I'm sure, will fill Santiago's new existence. Until now I'd kept the news to myself, but last night I told Lydia. She listened to my long monologue without interrupting even once. She felt (she confessed later) contradictory emotions. On the one hand, she was pleased by this mark of trust. I think that from tonight on, she murmured, we've grown closer, I think we're a couple now. Maybe. But she was also worried about me being so worried. She was silent for a while. She kept curling and uncurling one of her lovely black locks, and then said, Leave them to it, yes, leave them, don't get involved unless they ask you to, leave it to them and you'll see that life not only goes on, as you put it, but it settles down, it readjusts. Perhaps she's right. This earthquake has left us all limping, wounded, partially empty, sleepless. We'll never again be what we were. Each of us will have to decide if we're better or worse. Inside, and occasionally outside as well, we were in a storm, a hurricane passed over us and the calm we're enjoying now contains uprooted trees, collapsed roofs, torn-off TV antennae, and rubble, lots of rubble. Obviously, we have to rebuild ourselves: to plant new trees, but maybe we won't have the same shoots in our nurseries, the same seeds. It's fine for us to build new houses, but is it a good idea for the architect only to faithfully reproduce the previous plan? Wouldn't it be infinitely better for him to rethink the problem and draw a new plan, one that takes into account our current needs? To clear the rubble, as far as possible; because there will also be rubble that nobody can clear from their hearts or memory.

Extramural
(Fasten seat-belt)

the *fasten seat-belt* sign has been switched off, so I get my life back again and the stewardess is pretty/ when she hands me the orange juice I see her discreet pale pink fingernails that are so incredibly well-manicured/ I can tell she's a bit concerned about my beret but I'll take that off over my dead body

five years two months and four days and I still exist hurrah/ that makes one thousand eight hundred and eighty-nine nights bah

I'm so sleepy but I want to enjoy this huge change to the full/ to know I can do and undo the seat-belt and do it up again as often as I like while I listen to the murmur of the bumblebees/ none of the other three hundred passengers is enjoying the jet-engine bumblebees as much as yours truly here

the stewardess leaves me a newspaper and I ask her for another one/ she stares at the beret and leaves me two/ so there's a neutron bomb now the jails will still be standing but not the prisoners but also the millions and not the millionaires/ the schools will be there but not the schoolkids

but also the cannons and not the generals/ ah and the missile that leaves hamburg may fall on moscow but the response might not fall on hamburg but in oklahoma changes changes changes

I'm so sleepy yet I want to remember the faces of all my loved ones there/ the ones still there/ aníbal isn't a number esteban isn't a number ruben isn't a number/ they wanted to turn us into numbers but we screwed them we refused to become things/ esteban brother you've got enthusiasm for a good while yet/ you'll have to help those who don't have any/ ah but who'll help you?

so much hatred and yet I don't want to crumble into it lose myself in it/ during the first years I watered it daily as if it were an exotic plant/ then I understood I shouldn't pay them that homage and besides there was so much to think about plan analyse and do/ they're going to rot all by themselves aren't they?

they succeeded in driving andres mad/ perhaps it happened because he was too innocent had too much faith in mankind/ everything took him by surprise he always thought they've done all this but that must be an end to it/ they can't be so cruel but they were/ I'm going to convince them and he started to talk to them but they smashed his mouth/ he was too innocent that's why he went mad

from my neighbour's watch I know I slept more than an hour/ now I can think more clearly/ I feel fresh and decide to go to the toilet/ unbelievable this freedom to go to the toilet as often as you like/ my first piss as a free man/ here's to you

the man on my right is reading *time* and on my left is the aisle/ I wonder how I'll find the world's state of mind the formation and deformation of the world/ it would be too much bad luck that just when I get out the world explodes

my little beatriz what a party we're going to have/ the fact is I have no real idea what to expect/ obviously there's a problem I know there's a problem/ in her last letters graciela isn't the same but that doesn't mean I have to read between the lines/ sometimes I think she's sick and doesn't want to tell me/ or maybe the girl but I don't even want to think that beatriz what a party we'll have/ even dad has become enigmatic at first I thought it must be the censorship but not now

five years is a long time/ graciela is wonderful but exile is a gulf that grows deeper by the day/ graciela is wonderful and we have a lot of shared past and that counts/ of course I love her how wouldn't I but this slightly crazy doubt doesn't encourage love what's most likely is that I'm being unfair

dad replied in code when I told him about emilio/ he was intelligent but logically also a bit obscure although I get the impression that he really did understand and I'm better now I don't dream about the emilio of leapfrog or jacks any more/ aníbal talked a lot about him without knowing any of the details of course/ he suffered directly at his hands/ it seems he was a monster through and through

so nice a sound the humming bees/ ladies and gentlemen I'm flying the stewardess smiles at me I smile at her/ maybe my beret startled her but I'm not going to take it off not on your life/ what would the old lady have thought of all this/ perhaps it's best she didn't see or sense it/ she didn't talk a lot but she did talk to me/ between her and the old man there was a no man's land but occasionally they crossed it sometimes it was him and sometimes her/ the old man was always a bit taken aback and with good reason but she used to tell me in strict secrecy how much she loved him/ always making me swear never to open my mouth about it/ lovely old lady my old lady I still miss her after these five years of winter no one is going to steal the spring from me

springtime is like a mirror but mine has a broken corner/ it was inevitable it wasn't going to stay intact after this pretty full five years/ but even with a broken corner the mirror is useful spring is useful

that canny neruda once asked in one of his odes/ now spring tell me what you're for and who you're for good job I remembered/ what you're for/ I'd say to rescue us from any deep well/ the word itself is like a childhood ritual/ and who are you useful for well in my humble opinion you're useful for life/ for example simply by saying spring I feel viable courageous alive

it seems I must have moved my lips when I said spring because the passenger on my right is looking at me terrified/ poor guy/ I get the impression he only knows how to say winter/ and anyway I could have been praying/ people still do that on planes

a broken mirror/ maybe the new graciela broke it the distant graciela but that must be a crazy idea and she'll be waiting for me at the airport with little beatriz and dad/ everything will start up again normally naturally even though the springtime mirror is broken yes of course it must be

as soon as I can I'll buy myself a watch

the stewardess hands me the tray with the meal on it and given my evident poor post-dungeon state I ask only for a coke not as an ideological concession but because it's free/ salad with cockles-steak-peaches in syrup/ my mouth fills with disbelieving saliva/ the little knife is pretty I'd like to keep it and feel I am a common criminal

thinking it over it's not such a bad thing that in her last letters graciela has been withdrawn and distant/ I'll bring her close again/ first off I'll kiss her/ how often we used to have slanging matches and say really stupid and harsh things to each other and then we'd stare at one another in amazement I'd go over and kiss her and the world would be back in its place/ order would return to the world or rather a splendid disorder/ but even so for a long time while her mouth was covered by mine she would still be reproaching me for something or other but increasingly more gently and more softly until it was nothing more than a murmur and finally she would return my kiss/ secondly I'll kiss her again/ the fact is I haven't kissed in five years/ that in itself is enough to drive anyone mad

five years two months and four days are probably too high a price to pay for a mistake/ that's almost an eighth of my life up to now/ I err therefore I exist saint augustine the mistaken/ I sometimes wonder what would have happened to me if I'd been a worker rather than a conspicuous member of the much-insulted third sector/ I'd have been put away just the same/ that's blindingly obvious/ but maybe I would have adapted better to let's say the food/ not to the machine because no one gets used to that/ let's see what difference there is between my class consciousness and a proletarian's class conscience after all I work as well but of course there's almost a tradition a family background/ aníbal is a prole and jaime too/ for the military they were numbers just the same as us/ they don't know the difference/ at least they should be taught that there are arabic numbers and roman ones/ by making us all equal we all learned and we really did become equal

it's obvious that a prole is always more secure and won't allow himself to be driven to the mental contortions we writhe around in/ but we can all be loyal when it comes down to it/ say I or so I think/ them maybe more naturally more modestly while we on the other hand provide a complicated explanation of the supposed sacrifice and pull out of our sleeve all the principles we have accumulated along the way/ going on and on about all the honourable reasons there are for staying silent proles don't complicate their lives so much/ they suffer that's all/ they stay silent and *ciao*

to return is a must but to what country to what uruguay/ that will have a broken corner as well and yet it will reflect more realities than when the mirror was intact/ we have to return but to what springtime/ it doesn't matter what a disastrous state it's in but I want to recover my springtime/ they buried it under dry leaves with televised snow a sweating santa claus with the students of mitrione with the world cup won and the world cup lost with under-developing consultants but what they don't know is that beneath those layers of shit the old and new springtime is still there maybe with a broken corner but with wheat fields and ombú trees and prohibited and authorized tangos and comrade artigas and songs of freedom and trade unions and flocks of sheep and revolts and provisional regulations and grass-roots committees and ungovernable people and the milky way and university autonomy and bitter *maté* and the plebiscite and the football terraces/ we have to return/ naturally/ and uruguay in a broken mirror will show without vanity that stump we have inherited and the world will listen will understand will respect it

they've cleared away the tray and now my knees are hurting a bit/ what a state I'm in if I'm even pleased my knees are aching

graciela's legs graciela's thighs graciela's little bush

what can my folk over there be doing now

while the gentle drowsy buzz of the bees continues the man with *time* has fallen asleep on my shoulder/ I thought I deserved a better fate/ fortunately the young girl to his right sneezes opportunely and loudly/ my neighbour wakes with a start and straightens up muttering sorry/ his *time* falls on my side and I hand it back to him/ in prison we could read *claudia* how big of them I don't know what the red cross is complaining about/ I ought to sleep but hope I don't rest on my neighbour's bony shoulder

I can't/ now it seems I can't get to sleep/ the thing is my beret itches but I swear I'm not going to take it off

I'll have to start again from zero like a new-born babe which I am/ the daring little hairs pushing up under the beret are like new-born babes

let's see what would I like to have/ time to be frank/ top priority a watch/ then a pen that works/ then how shameful embarrassing a table tennis set with a net and everything/ how we used to play in solís with silvio and manolo with maría del carmen as well she was really good that girl/ she always used the chinese grip and gave the ball a terrific spin/ not rolando/ rolando would look on condescendingly from the side and always come out with the same refrain/ I don't know *che* how such stupid and dialectical people can take that bit of celluloid crap seriously/ and between serves silvio would remind him look mao is a ping-pong champion/ that's why I could never be a maoist rolando would say/ don't distraaaact me maría would shout you have to concentrate at this like you do in chess/ like in chess and *in coitus interruptus* said rolando, blowing out smoke/ pig you faat pig maria would yell again don't distraaact me skinny stan laurel here has already won five points off me/ but neither silvio nor I could ever beat her by more than twenty-one to nineteen

and I also want to talk and listen and talk and listen/ no more of those interrupted dialogues with aníbal or esteban that sometimes lasted two months split into four half-hour sessions/ thirty minutes every fortnight during the exercise period

rolando's a great guy/ with his tangos and his conquests/ always gadding about until he became politicized or rather we politicized him but then he was rock solid/ he called himself a convinced bachelor/ who knows if he's still undefeated/ he's going to fall going to fall/ how can I describe him /elegant lumpen / a crazy gent/ manolo used to say he was a duke fallen on hard times and in the end we all called him duke and whenever he got airs and graces he would order *endive* salad or *niente* so silvio completed his title and from then on he was the duke of *endives*/ he used to love it/ once in el chajá he was presented to the recently imported wife of a norwegian diplomat he kissed her hand and murmured very politely despite being in tattered shorts and rope sandals the duke of endives at your service madame although for the poor scandinavian woman it could have been pure chinese

my knee is still hurting/ it must be the threat of rheumatoid arthritis again/ but now I'll do gymnastics and after the six square metres I've been in any pigsty will be a palace

I'm happy/ I don't know if it shows but I'm happy/ I hope it doesn't show/ the man on my right will think I'm a pirate a mid-air hijacker/ I'm a landlubber mister don't worry a landlubber/ how strange the only pirates who've become completely anachronistic are sea pirates/ sandokan* incorporated and associates

the friends for heaven's sake/ silvio never again but I'll find rolando and manolo/ well it seems the duke is in mexico/ fantastic/ manolo in gothenburg/ he's split up with tita/ they're probably both right/ they're not to blame/ it's this earthquake that has shaken us all/ and besides exile saps your strength grinds you down/ exile is a torture machine as well/ you have to put the blame for all the frustration and anguish on somebody and of course the person who gets it is the one next to you, whoever is closest/ I hope graciela and I

I'd also love to see the sea

when all's said and done I came out better than when I went in/ that first little week/ ok that's enough enough enough/

* Sandokan is the hero otherwise known as the 'Tiger of Malaysia' in a series of swashbuckling adventure stories for children written by the Italian writer Emilio Salgari (1862–1911). His novels were translated into many different languages, becoming particularly popular in Portugal, Spain and Spanish-speaking parts of Latin America, such as Uruguay and Argentina.

I'm the same but am another person too/ and this other person is better/ I like this other person that I've become

springtime isn't yet within my reach/ spring will not arrive tomorrow but perhaps the day after/ reagan with his neutron bomb and stubborn as a mule but he won't be able to prevent spring arriving the day after tomorrow

that armpit smell isn't coming from me

a profound thought/ right now latin american unity is driven by two essential things/ reagan and the letter zed/ from the rio grande down to tierra del fuego we reject the dummy and we don't pronounce the zed/ so we don't despize him we despise him

ah but the other unity the one that isn't a joke/ of course being in jail unites puts an end to all cracks/ but that can't be the ideal formula/ it seems to me

sometimes I was afraid why deny it/ a fear whose howls I had to silence/ not one but many fears/ the fear of despising myself of preferring to die to give up on the world/ with no world and no balls/ the fear of ending up a wreck/ it's horrible to feel so afraid but even more horrible to have to silence your howls

afterwards the fear abated and it seemed incredible to have even brushed against it/ I could feel myself to be so brave and stoical afterwards/ and I was so transformed I could even feel a certain disdain/ for someone else who was afraid and had to swallow his howls/ someone who at some point if they didn't howl would get beyond that shitty moment and feel so brave and stoical they could even sense a certain disdain towards another person who in the jaws of his fear had to swallow his impulse to howl, and so on and so on

fear is the worst abyss and you can only get out of the pit by seizing your own hair and pulling upwards/ gradually you learn to lose fear of fear/ very gradually/ if you face it fear slinks away

the stewardess with the pale pink nails comes round offering headsets for those who want to see the film/ but they're not on the house/ they cost two dollars fifty cents and I'm stony broke or a broken stone it's the same/ and I say no as if I only wanted to sleep/ maybe I do

sadness is to be feared as well/ not merely your own but other people's/ what to do for example with a cellmate a big burly guy who all of a sudden shudders and sobs in the midst of the eternal darkness of night in prison/ how can you know what he's remembering or missing or regrets or is withstanding/ this fraternal sobbing soaks you like a persistent drizzle it's impossible to shelter from/ and as soon as you're bone-drenched your own personal sadnesses start to kick in/ sadnesses are like cocks/ one of them starts to crow/ and all the others follow suit/ and its only then you realize how enormous the collection is and that you even have some that are doubles

the film is about pianists/ it must be something about an international competition for promising young musicians/ with no sound it doesn't look like music but gymnastics/ both of them are pianists/ the neat and tidy girl and the dishevelled young man/ in the first half she's the one who dominates and they give each other neat little kisses but in the second he dominates and they give each other dishevelled ones/ and here am I who hasn't given anyone a neat or dishevelled kiss in five years/ of course the film is north american but one of the pianists in the competition must be soviet because she's always accompanied by two of those actors of scottish ancestry who used to play nazis and now are russians and besides the young girl's teacher scandalously asks for asylum even though this means she has to put aside the tremendous affection she feels for her pupil prodigy who due to the malign influence of marxism–leninism is a robot with tresses/ the final is incredibly hard-fought but victory goes to the western christian keyboard/ piano piano

the silent concert has made me sleepy/ it's incredible to see how on the small screen they're pounding away at the instrument and meanwhile you're deaf as a post/ there's no one so deaf as the one who wants to hear

there's also the idea of death/ it comes and goes/ sometimes it coincides with fear sometimes it doesn't/ in my case it usually didn't/ in the end pain creates more fear than death/ you can even see death as the

definitive analgesic but there's always some corner of springtime that resists

I really want to sit down for a week to chat with dad/ I want to talk to him about everything I didn't say in earlier years/ to hear what he has learned over these years and also for him to know what I've learned/ we think differently about many things but finding out about those differences is also a way to reduce them

for five years the most encouraging thing was the sun

how distant are childhood secondary school student struggles work wages/ they seem to belong to someone else/ sometimes I can even remember all the details but as if someone had told me them one foggy night

it was in buenos aires when little beatriz couldn't yet talk it was in buenos aires when graciela said I can't imagine not having you/ one rainy evening walking down calle lavalle snuggled together to take advantage of the only umbrella when a flood of argies came out of the cinemas

to me the only proof of god's existence are graciela's legs

in prison many of them turned their hand to writing verses/ not me/ what I did was sing tangos with the volume off quiet quiet in complete silence and how good they sounded not a single wrong note

in order not to betray never to give in you have to raise a stockade and be aware that even suffering even fearful even vomiting the stockade has to be defended to the death/ thank you john ford

when you are free and anxious you suddenly feel imaginary pains and think they are real/ in prison its different/ when you feel a real pain you have to think its imaginary/ sometimes that helps

outside to feel solidarity you have to bring together a thousand people and collect funds and denounce abuses and human rights/ inside on the other hand solidarity can be the size of half a cracker when its the corporals or sergeants who are looking through the slit to keep an eye on us I never wake up I don't pay them any attention/ I only wake up with a start when after those two its the officers who sneak a look at us

what if I reach the airport and there's nobody waiting for me/ no none of that/ best start again/ let's imagine that graciela and dad and little beatriz will be there

to play a game of volleyball or football was as important as founding a dynasty or discovering the law of gravity

altogether I was kept in solitary twenty days/ from there in other words from the famous hole you come out either crazy or stronger/ I came out stronger but the problem is I didn't discover the method

the stewardess moves so silently among the passengers that almost all of them wake up and say they're sorry and glance down nervously at their flies/ in some countries they call it a zipper/ the young woman who's on the right of the man on my right is literally sleeping sprawled out and from a pocket of her pretty jacket I can see half of a fork/ a common criminal

it's starting to become bumpy/ fasten seat-belt/ everyone wakes up/ the sprawling young woman unsprawls and promptly hides the fork

my stomach heaves as well but I'm happy all the same/ this is no moment or occasion to throw up/ my stomach is in my throat and the two of them greet each other how are you how are you/ their farewell is moving too for obvious reasons I had no visits/ that's bad but not so bad/ when you have visits you're anxious the whole week/ you try without success not to risk the slightest sanction/ you wait for that glimpse of your family/ as if it were magic and sometimes it is/ on the other hand/ when you don't have any visits you don't care about any sanctions/ you feel miserably alone/ but also freer or less of a prisoner

when I was nine more or less the same age as little beatriz now there were two things that holidays were good for/ one was to sit at siesta-time on the marble steps with my bottom nice and cool and read and read/ that was how I got through all verne and salgari and even tarzan and the apes/ in fact at school our secret password was kagoda/ and the other was to go to my aunt and uncle's smallholding on the coast/ between nine and fourteen I went there every summer/ there were no other kids around so I had to make do on my own and I would escape down to the river/ I told graciela in a letter or maybe in a planned letter or in a poor monologue with myself how I would get into the rowing boat and row to the centre of the river but on other occasions I would stay on the bank or lie under some enormous trees or at least that's how they looked to me and everything was a discovery the mushrooms the wood lice or a pair of filthy dogs who once fornicated right in front of me although I was unaware of what their gymnastics meant/ and remained stuck there with sad resigned faces/ I felt I was at the very centre of the universe and would have liked to know the secret of every tree bark every centipede every kiskadee and I didn't move because I knew that only by staying completely still would I have any chance of discovering the true intimacy of that mini-jungle/ and curiously it never occurred to me to shout kagoda because I knew that tarzan's ultimatum was not worth anything there nobody would have understood or been affected by his call to surrender/ and into that reality very early one morning there appeared a certain strange being although later I discovered he had much more right to be part of the landscape than I did/ he was a young boy but he was barefoot and dressed in rags/ his face legs and arms were covered in a layer of grime that seemed to me universal/ I was a bit frightened because lost in my daydreams I hadn't heard him approach or maybe I thought the noise among the branches was caused by the usual stray dogs and seeing I was afraid he chuckled laughing almost in spite of himself and sat down opposite me on a tree trunk/ occasionally shaking his head or swatting his hands to ward off the bluebottles/ I asked if he was from round there and he puffed out his cheeks again/ I didn't know what to do or what initiative I could take until it occurred to me to pick up a stone and with a great effort the greatest I could muster I threw it towards the river where it fell by the shore next to the rowing boat/ then he smiled again, blew his cheeks out stood up and also picked up a stone and almost effortlessly with his arm by his side also threw it into the river and that tiny pebble not only reached an incredible distance but bounced across the water almost without any ripples I could feel my chest swelling with admiration and I told him that's great and clapped and laughed and I don't know what else to show how he had astonished me and in the end I said you're a champ/ and he looked at me this time without puffing out his cheeks and spoke for the first time/ I'm not a champ because that's the only thing I can do

thanks to this backdrop of countryside memories and remote childhood I think I'm finally drifting off/ I'm going to count goons to see if I fall asleep

there it goes again *fasten seat-belt*/ ok ok/ I must have slept a couple of hours/ the bad thing is I dreamt again of emilio

Beatriz
(Airports)

An airport is a place where lots of taxis arrive and sometimes it's full of foreigners and magazines. In airports it's always so cold they put in a pharmacy to sell medicines to people who are susceptible. I've been susceptible since I was a little girl. In airports people yawn almost as much as they do in schools. In airports suitcases always weight twenty kilos so they don't really need weighing machines. In airports there are no cockroaches. There are in my house because it's not an airport. Football players and presidents are always photographed in airports and their hair looks well groomed, but matadors are hardly ever photographed, and still less bulls. It must be because bulls like travelling by train. I like that a lot as well. The people who go to airports are very huggy. When you wash your hands in airports they come out much cleaner but all wrinkled. I've got a little friend who steals loo paper from airports because she says it's softer. The customs and the luggage trolleys are the most beautiful things in an airport. At the customs you have to open your suitcase and shut your mouth. The air stewardesses walk in pairs so they don't get lost. The stewardesses are much prettier than primary school teachers. Their husbands are called pilots. When a passenger arrives late at the airport, there's a policeman who puts a stamp in his passport which says this child arrived late. Among the things that sometimes arrive at the airport is for example my father. The passengers who arrive always bring presents for their beloved daughters but my daddy who's arriving tomorrow won't bring me any present because he was a political prisoner for five years and I'm very understanding. We go to airports especially when my father is coming. When an airport is on strike it's much easier to find a taxi for the airport. There are some airports that as well as taxis have aeroplanes. When the taxis are on strike the planes cannot land. Taxis are the most important part of an airport.

The Other

(For now, improvise)

By now, Rolando Asuero is no longer posing himself questions. He's battled his way to a response, and for now he's totally convinced. All he has to do is go to the airport and confront the past, present and the future all bundled up together. Probably Graciela is right and the best thing will be to improvise. To improvise on a certain theme, of course. But what is he to do when Santiago arrives and embraces her and little Beatriz as being the reason as well as the unreason that keeps him alive. What to do? Where to put his hands? Where should he look? What to do when Santiago hugs Rafael and his dad strokes the back of his neck briefly because that's a gesture that his retreating generation make. And above all, what on earth to do when Santiago gives him a hug and says, How great you're here, Duke, I was thinking of you on the plane, we'll have to start reuniting the old clan, what d'you reckon? And what will Graciela's expression be when in the middle of the hug he peers over Santiago's shoulder at her? Yet Rolando thinks the worst moments will come later, when Graciela finally tells Santiago and the new arrival begins to relive the scene at the airport and sees how stupid he was and despises himself and us as well because we all knew the score apart from him, and when he starts replaying the kisses he gave Graciela in front of me and the hug he gave me in front of Graciela, and it's going to be very hard for him to get over that fleeting moment that took

place only a few hours earlier. How to convince him that
nobody planned it, it just happened, that the old comradeship
the seven of them had developed turned out to be a breeding
ground for them to grow closer and in the end to love one
another. Because it is love, Santiago, it's not just a fling, that's
what's good and bad about it, thinks Rolando, that's what in
the end humanly justifies Graciela and me, but which also
makes Santiago the definitive loser. Definitive? One logical
question is whether he'll give in or fight, if he'll accept the most
obvious facts or if, playing the intelligent card and staying
calm, he'll say to Graciela, OK, let's not decide anything right
now, remember I've only just got here, straight out of prison
and I've got to get used, not only to this new situation, but to
the world in general, it'll be better if we talk, though probably
not all three of us, just we two who lived through so much
jointly playing the piano with our four hands, why should we
rush to settle everything when we've got all the time in the
world ahead of us, before we settle things let me enjoy little
Beatriz for a while, let me have long talks with her, don't worry,
not about this problem, the last thing I want is for the image
she has of you to suffer, and I'll talk to Rolando as well, but
later on, for now everything seems so incredible to me and I
keep thinking I'll wake up from dozing off again on the plane.
Obviously, this is a fairly accurate variation, especially knowing Santiago as I do, because when he decides to stay calm he
usually succeeds, and here it's more than simply a question of
not losing his calm but his wife as well. Rolando also thinks
that would be what he would do if he were Santiago. For now,
he tugs a sideburn and arches his eyebrows. He'd like everything to reach its climax as quickly as possible. In reality, it's
Graciela who has to make the final decision, because both Santiago on one side and he on the other want to be with her, sleep
with her, live with her. And possibly it's here that he, Rolando

Asuero, enjoys a slight advantage over Santiago, because he is aware that when it comes to bodily semantics Graciela and he have such a close understanding, besides which of late she has often given him the tender certainty – no, the almost ferocious certainty – that she is going to continue with him and not with Santiago. But Santiago's advantage might be regarded as little Beatriz, because if, depending on what happens and what decisions are taken, Santiago wants to take her with him, Rolando is not so sure that Graciela, who is a lion of a mother, would easily accept giving up her child, someone who logically in addition is dazzled by a father who has spent five years in prison and is a complete novelty to her. Then again, Rolando Asuero tells himself on the way to the airport, is it a situation that may not be ideal, but is at least reasonable? What real benefit would Santiago get from such a forced union, where the kid was nothing more than a pawn in a game of blackmail? Of course, he doesn't like that word; he admits it shows a lack of respect towards Santiago, and he mentally decides to remove it from the equation. But human beings are so unpredictable. It could also be that Santiago prefers to continue with Graciela in a diminished relationship than to see Graciela in bed with another man, even if this other man is a soulmate, or precisely because of that far from negligible detail. All right, here's the airport at last, and as he descends from the bus Rolando is so caught up in his thoughts he almost misses a step.

Extramural
(Arrivals-Arrivées-Llegadas)

strange I feel strange walking on this ground/ just as well it's raining/ the rain makes everything the same and the umbrella becomes humanity's common denominator/ at least of sheltered humanity

I feel strange, but that will pass/ no one dies of strangeness although they can die of becoming estranged/ it was too much all at once/ the news/ the saying goodbye to people there/ the ridiculous red tape/ the triumphant smile of the last official but one/ carrasco/ departure with no one accompanying me/ the journey the long journey with dreams and doubts and plans/ oh and the meals/ of course it felt strange after five years of that disgusting slop

the official studying the document for ages/ the truth is that four minutes can be an eternity/ please take your beret off and then a careful comparison with the photograph/ still serious but very pally so you're another one/ yes another one/ I respond in kind/ only then a smile and his stern face changes into a that of a puckish little indian/ good luck my friend/ good luck friend he told me now I have to wait for the luggage/ my poor case will arrive or will not/ this is going to take time/ and all those people waiting/ there are so many heads on the far side of the glass/ if only I could see them/ find them

yes, there they are/ it's them of course it is/ *uruguayans our fatherland or our tomb*/ workers of the world unite/ eureka/ there's only one sky-blue flag/ *fiat lux*/ *nosce te ipsum*/ fatherland or death we will overcome/ long live those who fight/ shit how happy I am

graciela and dad and that lovely little thing who must be my kid/ graciela the beautiful/ to think that's my wife/ little beatriz, what a party we're going to have/ and who's that other one raising his arms? /why if it isn't the duke/ it's the duke of endives in person

Palma de Mallorca, October 1980–October 1981

20/04/18